I0687410

Gift Wrapped

a sweet & spicy christmas romance

karla doyle

GIFT WRAPPED

After catching her boyfriend cheating two weeks before Christmas, Brinn is seriously lacking in holiday spirit. So when she looks into the eyes of a last-minute shopper after closing on Christmas Eve, she's sarcastic rather than sympathetic. But Brinn is ever the good girl and her conscience wins out. She offers the handsome stranger ten minutes to select a gift and ends up with a present of her own—a date. On Christmas Eve.

Davis hates Christmas. Especially this year, since a neighborhood heist liberated him of his hard-earned belongings and the few gifts he'd purchased. But the robbery led him to a cute store manager with a sense of humor, smokin' body and no plans for the evening. Mistletoe might be in order after all.

Their Christmas Eve date is like gift-wrapped, sexy satisfaction. But the best gifts keep on giving, and one naughty night may not be enough—for either of them.

*To my amazing family, fabulous friends
and wonderful readers...thank you!
Without your love and support,
this book wouldn't exist.*

*Extra hugs to Todd, Amanda, Andie,
Grace, Claire R., and L.*

Chapter One

BRINN

CLOSING TIME, FINALLY. AS MUCH AS BRINN enjoyed her job, standing behind a roll-down door, folding sweaters and tagging merchandise wasn't her ideal Christmas Eve.

Not that she had anywhere special to be. Catching her snake of an ex-boyfriend with his pants around his ankles and his dick in another woman's mouth had vaulted Brinn to the top of the "newly single" column. With everybody she cared about two hours' drive away —in good weather—she was the definition of solo this holiday season. Might as well put in time here, prepping for the Boxing Day sale, rather than hurry "home" to her empty apartment. Christmas really sucked it this year.

She ducked behind the counter and killed the loop

of festive tunes. She'd loved holiday songs her entire life, however, eight to ten hours of merry music every day for two solid months tended to squeeze the last drop of festive spirit from your soul. Thank god she'd said her last, politically correct, "Have a great holiday" for this year.

She straightened, surveyed the chaotic state of the small chain store she managed, and looked into the face of a dreaded beast—the solitary male with an unfinished shopping list.

There was one every year. Usually a mid-fifties man with desperate, pleading eyes and a frown because he'd just realized—at closing time on Christmas Eve—that he didn't have enough gifts under the tree. This year's last-minute shopper didn't look more than mid-thirties, tops. A hint of anxiety played on his face, but it didn't diminish his good looks. Shaved head, strong jaw, warm eyes. Wide shoulders filling out a black cargo-style jacket. Very nice.

His fingers curled around the rungs of the metal roll-down door. He flashed a charming smile to go with the eye contact.

Good try, buddy, but it is so *not happening.*

Didn't matter how attractive he was, Brinn didn't return the smile. That'd only encourage him. Instead, she gave him a view of her back and resumed setting the store to rights.

Apparently dude missed the memo on interpreting body language, because the metal rattled behind her.

Thirty seconds later, he lightly shook it again. Seriously, he thought that'd work?

"We closed at five." She tossed the words over her shoulder. Best acknowledgement he was going to get.

"Yeah, you and the rest of the world."

Exactly. *Now get moving.* Too bad she couldn't say that out loud.

"Look, I know I'm late, but I only need one more thing. It's kind of an emergency."

She shook her head, hoping to hell he saw it. "Sorry, can't help you. The superstore on Fourth Avenue is open until seven tonight for *emergencies* like this. Perfume is a lovely gift—I recommend Acqua di Gioia by Giorgio Armani." The very thing she'd hoped to get from Liam. The idiot had bought it, she'd found it tucked between his t-shirts. He'd just put another woman's name on the gift tag for tomorrow. Lousy jerk.

"Thanks for the suggestion, but the person I'm shopping for doesn't wear perfume."

Well la-de-da for her. Brinn sighed and rattled off the next item on her personal wish list. "You can't go wrong with chocolates. The Lindor balls wrapped in foil are my personal favorite. Especially the white-chocolate kind."

A deep laugh rumbled from the other side of the metal mesh. "Good to know."

Brinn smiled at the comment. The pushy guy had a nice laugh and a sexy voice, she'd give him that much.

"Look, I've already closed off the register...I couldn't sell you anything if I wanted to."

"I have cash. I'll be fast and I'll give you a big tip at the end."

"Wow, that's quite the proposition. I know my skirt's a little on the short side, but I'm not that kind of salesgirl." She waited, but sexy-voice guy didn't say another word. Or rattle the cage.

She half-turned to sneak a peek. Gone. Which *should* be a relief, but stirred her guilt instead. Her disappointment too.

She moved to the door and spotted him three stores down, walking away. "Hey," she called. No answer— except from her conscience. Ah, crap. She turned the lock and rolled the door up enough to scoot underneath. Biggest mistake ever, coming right up. Well, second biggest. Moving out here to be with Liam currently held the number-one spot.

She did a ridiculous, high-heeled jog past several darkened stores. The sound of her heels echoed in the quiet mall, but the guy still didn't look back. "Hey, wait up," she said again, once she had him within arm's reach.

He stopped so abruptly that she plowed into him. And bounced off, because he was *that* solid. Oh boy. Now that they were face-to-face, without the benefit of a heavy-duty metal screen separating them—or any witnesses to speak of—he was a bit intimidating. Not super tall or monstrously built, but she didn't doubt for a minute he was capable of kicking some serious ass.

"I, um..." Dry mouth plus empty brain much? His intense stare didn't help matters. She cleared her throat and tried again. "C'mon back and I'll try and help you find something for your wife."

"I'm not married."

"Okay, for your girlfriend."

His jaw ticked. The corners of his mouth lifted in a sexy half grin. "Not shopping for one of those, either."

Awareness zinged her, heating her cheeks and making her nipples tingle before settling between her legs. "Sister, aunt, granny, roommate, long-lost childhood friend you recently reconnected with on Facebook...whoever she is, I'm giving you ten minutes to find her a gift from my seriously depleted stock. Take it or leave it."

"I'll take it. Thank you." His genuine, full-face smile nearly melted her knees out from under her.

"Great."

"You're really saving me here."

She flapped a hand at him as they walked. "No problem. Glad to help." Clearly she'd had too much stale mall air. This after-hours personal-shopping stint would likely set her back thirty minutes, not ten. She still had the daily reports to complete and a couple hundred gaudy Boxing Day sale tags to attach. At this rate, it'd be close to seven o'clock before she flopped on her couch with a bowl of soup and the annual cable presentation of *Frosty the Snowman*.

Yet she still had a stupid smile plastered across her face. Good lord. A couple of weeks without a boyfriend had reduced her to this? Maybe it wasn't too late to send a note to Santa. Perfume and chocolates weren't the only things on her wish list.

She motioned her guest into the store. Corporate policy dictated she keep the door locked at all times outside of non-operating hours. Brinn paused, one hand on the metal. Close herself in with a total stranger? Screw the rules for once. The mall was a virtual ghost town. If the man standing in her disheveled store turned out to be a robber instead of a handsome last-minute shopper, she'd rather he had a quick exit route via an open door. Decision made.

She wiped her clammy palms on her skirt and joined him by a rack of hoodies and yoga pants. "Tell me what you had in mind and hopefully I can send you out of here with a smile on your face."

From the creases forming at the corners of his eyes, the words sounded as sexually suggestive to him as they did to her ears. Oh the awesomeness that flew out of her mouth sometimes.

"I think you can count on that happening..." His mischievous hazel eyes dropped to her nametag, then back. "Manager Brinn."

Top salesperson in her district for the past nine

months, yet hearing her name in his deep, smooth voice left her without a single intelligent thing to say.

The whole situation was crazy. Letting her assistant manager leave early, even though it meant closing and tackling the sale prep alone. Inviting a hot guy—who appeared to be unattached—into the store afterhours.

Maybe it wasn't crazy. Maybe it was one of those fated situations. Or maybe she needed a semi-nutritious meal and a day off really, really badly.

As casually as anything, he unzipped his coat and scrubbed one hand along his clean-shaven jaw. He smiled. Just a little one, but it warmed her all over. The man made no bones about checking her out. Top to bottom, not lingering over any one area, though his slow perusal indicated he appreciated the view.

Thank god she'd opted for her business-sexy look today, rather than slumming it in the comfier clothes the store sold. The short black skirt, sheer hose and strappy heels made her legs look long and lean, despite her shorter stature. Her crossover top's plunging neckline accented some decent cleavage. With her hair in an upsweep, she almost pulled off elegant—or she had nine hours ago, when everything was fresh.

As much as she'd love thirty seconds in front of a mirror with lipstick and a piece of dental floss, the clock was ticking. A security guard would be banging on her door at six o'clock, telling her to clear out, no exceptions. Because after all, who in their right mind would want to stay late at work on Christmas Eve? Only someone with no personal life whatsoever would sign up for that.

She pushed the self-pitying thought aside and reclaimed her voice. "Better start shopping, you're running down the clock." For show, she tapped her watch. "Santa's on his way. I need to get home to my bed so he'll sneak in and fill my stocking."

Her private shopper laughed and winked. "Santa has all the luck."

Oh. Dear. God. Was everything out of her mouth going to sound dirty? And holy, could he get any sexier than right now, smiling at her like a tomcat that'd caught a mouse? She'd have to make a stop at the superstore before it closed and buy a pack of triple-As for her battery-operated boyfriend.

"So, give me the specs on this not-a-wife, not-a-girl-friend, who doesn't wear perfume."

His hands disappeared into the front pockets of his jeans, taking her mind along with them. "I'd say Alicia's about your height and build, but younger, and less... curvy."

"All right. And on that note, guess I'll start my New Year's diet a week early and pray that Santa brings me some anti-aging cream." When he dared to chuckle, Brinn pulled a pair of black, size-small pants from the rack and stabbed them at him. A soft, white hoodie with lots of form-fitting seam details followed. "How about this set? It looks fantastic on trim, younger women."

He didn't even bother to look at the stuff. Just kept his gaze on her. "Do you like it?"

"I do. I have the same ones at home...slightly stretched out from my *curviness*."

This time, he was smart enough not to laugh. Might as well have, though, given the smile that spread across his face. "I bet it looks fantastic on you."

Uh-huh. Nice recovery.

"Can you pick a top to go with these?" he asked.

"Sure." One full-price t-shirt coming right up. "Accessories to match?"

"Go for it."

Yes, he was charming. Really good-looking too. But he was still getting a shopping bag full of add-ons for that "curvy" comment, and more so, for laughing about it.

Socks—check. A multi-pack, of course. Brinn paused with one hand on the hair accessories. "Does she have long hair?"

"Very."

"Great." Probably sleek and naturally blonde, unlike Brinn's defiantly wavy, chemically highlighted version. She gave him a false smile and added the obligatory black hairband. Then a second one in white. And a pair of earrings for the finish, the cheesiest ones left in stock. "How about these?"

He studied the three-inch danglers hanging from her fingertips. "No idea. I'm a guy, remember?"

As if she'd forget that. "Does she wear this type?"

"I've never noticed. If you think they're good, throw them in. I trust your judgment."

Dammit. Caught by the conscience clause. Back to the rack they went, to be replaced by medium-sized, silver hoops with a filigree pattern.

He caught her hand as she added them to the lot. "Those I like."

"Me too. I have the same pair."

"Yeah?" His thumb swept across her fingers, inciting a riot of electricity throughout her body.

She swallowed and nodded. "Ready for the damage?"

"Hit me." He let her hand slide free. Pressed his palms to the countertop and leaned in as close as the slab of heavily lacquered wood allowed.

She'd logged a lot of cash-register time in her years. Her current district manager called her "Fingers McIntyre" because of her speed and accuracy at the till. Except for now.

The weight of his gaze made her shaky, caused her fingers to bumble on the keys. A curse slipped out, under her breath, and he smiled again. Her cheeks burned like coals in a cozy Christmas fire, but she smiled back.

"Sorry about the language," she said. "I'm not used to making mistakes."

"Lucky you—I make them all the time."

"Like forgetting to buy Alicia a gift until closing time on Christmas Eve?"

"I didn't forget."

"Just lost track of time for the past few weeks?" Ouch, that came out snotty. Hopefully he'd think she was tired and eager to get home, not pick up on the wholly unjustified jealousy working its way through her system. "Sorry. Long day. Week, month..." She centered her attention on the enter button, jabbing it harder than necessary. "One hundred, fifty-six dollars and ninety-seven cents."

"Shit." He pulled the wallet from his back pocket. "More than I planned on spending. Hope I have that much cash."

"We take Interac and all the major credit cards." She sighed when he stopped poking through the bills and nailed her with a look. "Yes, I fibbed. I haven't closed off the debit machine yet. I'm severely behind schedule tonight."

He extended a Visa card, not relinquishing it until she gave in and met his eyes. "I apologize for holding you up. I'm keeping you from someone on an important night, I realize, but I really do appreciate you doing this for me. And Alicia."

"Nope, I'm flying solo in the sled this year." Over-sharing in progress...check.

"I assume that's by choice. A beautiful woman with a generous spirit and sense of humor could have her pick of Santas." The twinkle in his eyes matched the suggestive comment. Probably just the way he was with people. He couldn't really be hitting on her—not while he was shopping for somebody else, and somebody significant, obviously.

The sound of technology doing its thing pulled her focus from his face. Paper scrolled from the machine, meaning her time was almost up. She slid the receipt across the counter with a pen and watched him sign with a dramatic scrawl. Strong hands to go with the ultra-masculine everything else. A girl couldn't help but swoon a little.

"I hope Alicia realizes how lucky she is, having you as her Santa." There, she'd done it. Flirted with him. On purpose this time, even if he *was* presently signing the bill for another woman's gift.

A straight line replaced his smile. "I doubt she'll see it that way."

"Then she's crazy."

"No, she's not."

Whoever Alicia was, she'd stolen the amazing smile from his face, therefore, she was an idiot. He'd said he wasn't shopping for a girlfriend, but that didn't mean he didn't wish otherwise. What kind of bitch must Alicia be, keeping a man like this on a string?

Brinn wanted to follow him home so she could give this Alicia person a slap. Having somebody toy with your heart sucked. Massively. Exhibit A in that category —Liam. The bastard. He never went out of his way for anybody. His own selfish desires always took priority.

Yet she'd been blind to it. Naively looked the other way because she wanted the relationship to last. When he'd suggested she request a transfer and move out here to be with him, she'd believed he'd changed, that he wanted the same thing.

The joke was still on her about that one. He'd proven his level of commitment when moving day had rolled around—by going to a ball game with a buddy rather than help her unload the van. The guy currently returning her pen wouldn't do something like that. She felt it in her soul.

"I hope Alicia likes the outfit," she said, sliding the bag across the counter. "But I put a gift receipt in there just in case. She has sixty days if she needs to exchange or return anything."

"I'll let her know."

"Have a great holiday." The words came out flatter than a week-old can of cola.

"Yeah, you too." His voice gave hers a run for first place in the lack-of-enthusiasm department.

She turned the key in the register and started the end-of-day process, then followed him to the front of the store, where she rolled the door into place for the second time today. If the past twenty minutes had done one thing, it was convince her there were still quality men out there. As soon as head office finalized her transfer request and she settled in a different city, she'd start searching for one. Again. Next Christmas, maybe she'd have a Santa to call her own. For good.

Her favorite customer of *this* holiday season stopped before he got six feet away. He turned quickly, meeting her wistful gaze. Shit. Busted. Thank goodness she'd likely never see him again.

"Did you forget something?" she asked, doing her best to sound like a store manager, not president of the local lonely-hearts club.

"I know it's Christmas Eve, but do you want to do something tonight?"

"What about Alicia? Don't you have plans with her?"

"Yeah, but that'll only take five minutes."

"Ouch. Is improving your stamina on your list of New Year's resolutions?"

His gut-deep laugh echoed through the empty mall corridor. Then, alpha as hell, he stalked back to the door. The metal separating them would probably bend if he touched it, the man was so damn hot.

"I don't do resolutions, but if I did, improving my stamina wouldn't need to be one of them."

She believed him with every sexually charged cell in her body. She still wasn't falling for another player's games, regardless of his considerable charm. "Alicia might argue that claim, given the five-minutes thing."

"Alicia's my fourteen-year-old neighbor."

"Oh. Sorry. I assumed...oh crap."

He smiled again, this one complete with creases at the corners of his eyes and a twinkle in his hazel irises. "Don't worry about it. I like your fiery comebacks."

"You'd love me when I have PMS, I'm extra fiery then." Yes, she'd just suggested he *love* her. And she'd mentioned her period. To a sexy stranger. Dear god. He should be running away in three, two—

"How much longer 'til you're free of this cage?" he asked, curling his fingers around the metal rungs.

"Mall security will come along to kick me out at six o'clock."

"And after that—any plans?"

"Fuzzy pajamas, canned soup and an animated snowman."

"Any chance you'd be willing to make substitutions?"

Brinn resisted the urge to jump up and down while making excited, squealing-type noises. "There's a possibility, yes. What did you have in mind?"

"A late dinner at my house. I'll cook and clean up. You just sit there and give me something pretty to look at. After that, a non-animated Netflix movie of your choice."

Oh wow. He was good. Too good to be true, probably. And hopefully not an ax murderer disguised as a handsome last-minute shopper. Well, she'd leave a note in her apartment just in case. So the cops knew where to find her sexy bald killer if she failed to show up for Christmas dinner tomorrow. Tonight, she was taking a leap of faith.

"What about my fuzzy pajamas? You don't have any substitutions to suggest for those?"

His gaze slid down her body, nice and slow. When his eyes returned to her face, they'd deepened to a rich golden-brown. "Plenty of suggestions. But I'll take you however you're dressed."

Or undressed, as she bet the case would be. She was one syllable away from agreeing to what could be the sexiest Christmas Eve of her life...with a total stranger. "I don't even know your name."

His eyebrows rose. "Aren't you supposed to verify my signature against the name on my credit card, Manager Brinn?"

Fire raced to her cheeks. Shit. How many times was he going to catch her off her game?

He winked while tapping his watch. "It's Davis. Davis Rourke. You'd better go finish up in there," he nodded toward her store, "you're running down the clock."

Chapter Two

DAVIS

TO HANG AROUND OR HEAD OUT—GOOD question. He'd written his phone number on the credit card receipt. If she didn't see it in her scramble to finish up, this opportunity might slip on by. Not a chance Davis was willing to take. Too much shit in the world fell into the can't-be-controlled column. Getting to know the cute store manager wasn't going to be one of those things.

So he sat. And waited. Far enough down the empty corridor not to creep her out. Close enough to keep an eye on the front of her store. If she came out looking for him, he'd step up. If it seemed as if she was making a break for it, he'd chalk it up to a worthy attempt and spend Christmas Eve alone. Same as always.

Brinn had disappeared from his view for fifteen

minutes. Since returning to the front section of the store, she'd kept busy folding and tidying merchandise. Every time she leaned over, a section of curly, dirty-blonde hair that'd escaped her clip fell over her eye. She'd huff at it and tuck it behind her ear, just to have it fall again the next time she leaned over. Very cute.

She looked pretty with her hair up. Didn't mean he couldn't wait to see it down, loose and tumbling around her shoulders, where he could comb his fingers through it until she sighed in relaxation, or wrap it around his fist while he made her moan.

He shifted on the slatted metal bench, opening his legs wider to accommodate his growing situation. She'd be out in less than ten minutes—still plenty of time to things under control. If he stopped watching her. Yeah, as if that was going to happen.

Pretty face with expressive, blue eyes and a smile that fried every nerve ending in his body. A long, slender neck with wisps of hair curling at the nape, begging to be swept aside so he could lick his way up and down the creamy skin. And those legs...Jesus. The shape of her calves, the curve of her thighs where they disappeared under the short, tight skirt. Her legs were what'd caught his attention first, what he'd been staring at when she noticed him standing outside her store. He'd almost forgotten about buying a gift.

Time to think about something other than how good she'd smelled when he'd gotten close. Or the way her pupils had dilated and the pink that'd spread across her cheeks when she'd flirted with him, intentionally and otherwise.

Shit, more blood heading south. He cracked his neck side to side. Didn't help. Even with half the blood in his body now residing in his cock, his brain still worked, and it wouldn't stop tormenting him with scenarios. How her lips would part when he kissed her. How her skin would taste when he explored every inch.

If he didn't get his mind out of the bedroom immediately, he'd be walking bowlegged when he escorted her from the mall.

She spent the remaining minutes buzzing around the store at a speed that would've given a cyclone a run for its money. She'd probably been on her feet all day—hell, for weeks on end, given the time of year—yet she worked her way through the store with more energy than most people had on a good day. Energy like that could certainly be put to more pleasurable use.

A security guard approached Brinn's store at an agitated clip, his pasty face screwed into a scowl. The sight of Brinn leaning over a table of sweaters had him changing gears, though. He came to a full stop outside the roll-down door, cocked his head and zeroed in on Brinn's ass. The fucker even grabbed his junk and did a couple of quick passes over top of his gray uniform pants.

Call him a hypocrite or whatever, Davis didn't care. No cop-wannabe was going to sneak up on Brinn and objectify her that way. Not while he was around.

He was on his feet and practically on top of the idiot in about three seconds. "Hey." He used his getting-shit-done voice to make his presence known to both the guard and Brinn. From her—a surprised smile. The dude, on the other hand, clenched his jaw. Even puffed his chest out. Bold move. Stupid, but bold.

Davis narrowed his eyes. *Bring it, jackoff.*

"Mall's closed. I'll show you to the nearest exit." The toy cop's gaze slid back to Brinn, taking a long, lewd look before returning to Davis. "Then I'll come back for her."

Like hell. Not in this guy's wildest dreams was that happening.

Davis shook his head slowly, cracked his knuckles and let his hands hang at his sides. "I'm waiting for the lady."

The idiot frowned, but made the wise choice to deflate. "Then get her and vacate the premises. It's time to clear out." Taking one last verbal stab at being the alpha dog, was he? Another mistake.

Davis had never lost a pissing match. He sure as hell wasn't starting now, with this loser. "When she's ready, that's when we'll go."

"Employee hours are done."

"Yeah? How long are you here tonight," he eyed the guy's identification badge, "Nelson?"

"Until midnight." Nelson cupped one hand around the holstered walkie-talkie, as a cop would a gun. "I'm the night *supervisor.*"

Such a lame, obvious attempt to impress Brinn. She bit into her bottom lip, clearly stifling the urge to laugh. Her amusement made this bullshit worthwhile. Also made it hard not to smile when he needed to appear menacing. Brinn's adorableness softened his edge, but not his cock. Time to switch tactics and get them out of here.

"You almost ready to call it a night, babe?" With that final word, he'd jumped them from strangers about to have a first date to an intimately familiar couple. For the benefit of the security douchebag, nothing else. Hopefully Brinn connected the dots on that one.

The mall cop's head swiveled to Brinn. She winked —directly at Davis. "Just need to turn off the lights and grab my purse, honey."

That shouldn't have sounded as good as it did. The word *babe* shouldn't have rolled off his tongue like melted butter, either. Must be the Christmas effect. And the break-ins. He'd come to the mall for something to make Alicia feel better, not to sign up for the beginning of something meaningful. Dinner, a movie, a mutually fulfilling romp in the bedroom—all yeses. A standing date every Saturday night and a box of tampons under his sink—hell no.

The neon sign flickered off first, followed by the interior lights as her store joined the rest in darkness. Brinn ducked under the door and brought it down with a clang. Then bent to lock it.

Thank you, shitty door design, for putting the deadbolts at floor level and providing him—and Nelson—with a primo view up the back of her short skirt.

He should've laid a fist to the security guard for ogling *his* woman. But he couldn't blame the guy. Not to mention, punching the idiot would've required Davis to tear his eyes from Brinn's ass, and that idea didn't appeal much.

Instead he issued the guard a low, "Merry Christmas" while both of them stared at Brinn's very fine can.

Nelson came back with, "Yours will be."

Davis chuckled under his breath. Yeah, it just might.

DAVIS

The security guard locked the heavy mall doors as soon as Davis and Brinn stepped through. With gusto, in fact. That left the two of them standing in the cold, under the sickly glow of fluorescent parking-lot lights. A little awkward, but nothing he couldn't handle. Brinn, on the other hand, looked ready to bolt, or possibly throw up.

So he did what was necessary to alleviate her stress. "Here's my info," he said, pulling a slightly weathered business card from his wallet. He scribbled his address and cell number on the back. Pressed it against her palm, putting the fate of their impromptu date in her hands, literally. "I'll watch from here until you're safely inside your car, then I'll head to mine. If I see you later, great. If not, it was nice meeting you, Brinn."

She nodded and walked away.

Forty minutes later, the headlights of a small car lit his bay window. She could've bailed—done the no-call, no-show. Or called and made an excuse. Anything would be feasible on Christmas Eve. She hadn't. However, she hadn't gotten out of her car yet, either.

Davis surveyed the situation from inside his house. The exterior light illuminated most of the driveway, giving him a good view of Brinn, sitting in her parked car, staring down at her lap. Her lips moved steadily. Talking via speakerphone? Singing along to her favorite song? Or having a conversation with an alternate personality about how she should dispose of his body after murdering him in his sleep tonight...

Trust issues still on board—hell yeah. Idiot. He had no reason to think Brinn was a nutcase like Linda. Or Terri. Besides, he'd learned his lesson. Relationships worked best when he stuck with the KISS method— Keep It Sexual and Short. Have a good time together, but get clear before emotional attachments formed. Two dates were usually safe. Three, max. Of course, to make it to a second or third date, there had to be a first. That wouldn't happen if Brinn didn't get out of the car.

He stepped out onto the small front stoop, kicking the fresh dusting of snow aside as he walked to the driveway. Their eyes connected and Brinn smiled at him through the windshield. Warm, friendly. Not the grin of a psycho female—he hoped.

"Checking in with somebody?" he asked when she exited her car. Because he couldn't just leave it alone.

"What? Oh, no. Talking to myself." She fiddled with the strap of her purse. Her eyes flitted everywhere but at him. "Talking myself down."

Shit. And the crazy-o-meter just spiked to the orange zone.

"We can rain-check dinner and the movie." He left off the *permanently* part, though it was right there, on the tip of his tongue. "No pressure, Brinn. Really."

Now, she looked at him. "No, it's just that..." No craziness in the eyes focused on him, just nervousness. "I've never, um, done...this." Pink colored her cheeks. Could've been from the cold, but he doubted it.

"That makes two of us."

With a hand planted on her jutted left hip and one eyebrow arched, she silently called bullshit.

He had to smile. Smile, and hope she didn't turn out to be batshit crazy once they were inside his house, because he was back to wanting her there. In his kitchen. Living room. In his bed if things went well.

"It's the truth. I've never picked up a woman in the mall, and I've never spent Christmas Eve with somebody I just met. See, never done this."

"Hmm."

"I had to make another stop on my way home, so I

haven't started dinner yet." He nodded toward his white-sided bungalow. "And I'm starving. You?"

"Very."

"Great. Come on." One hand under her elbow and the other at the small of her back, he guided her over the snow-covered path. "Sorry about this. Shoveled it before I left for work this morning, but it's been snowing all day and—"

"And after work you had to rush to the mall to rattle my door."

"Something like that." He turned the handle and motioned her through the opening. "Welcome. Sorry it looks like somebody trashed the place. That's because somebody trashed the place."

Brinn swiveled abruptly, bringing them face-to-face. "What?"

"Yeah, the bastards hit a couple of houses sometime this afternoon. Cleaned out all the wrapped presents, electronics and furniture, jewelry, whatever they could easily get out the door. Stuff that's easy to move and pawn. Cops said the same thing's been happening around the city the past week. Typical of the season."

She quickly surveyed the areas she could see. "How much of your stuff did they take?"

"Pretty much everything I just listed."

"Oh my god. And on Christmas Eve..." Her soft eyes searched his face. "They must've had a truck to do that. How'd they get in? And hit multiple places without somebody noticing?"

"Lady across the street saw what she thought was a furniture delivery truck in my driveway. Only my place and the house next door were hit. No fences separating our yards. Both houses had forced rear entries. Back-door jobs."

Her lips curved into the cutest hint-of-naughty smile he'd ever seen. "Sorry. It's horrible, not funny in the slightest, but..."

Half a step put them in very close proximity. "But?" He thumbed the zipper tab of her coat. Slid it down the track until the short, formfitting jacket hung open, revealing some very nice cleavage.

She shivered as he slid the black jacket from her shoulders and down her arms. "But that description was kind of, um...dirty. To me, anyway. But my mind always tends to head for the gutter."

Not a bad thing from where he stood. A lifetime of keeping his feelings in check had given him a killer poker face, which he put to use now. "What did I say that sounded dirty?"

"Come on, Davis." One eyebrow rose at him. "Think about it."

Oh, he was thinking about it all right. Hard not to think about rear entries with the memory of Brinn's upturned ass in that tight little skirt imprinted on his brain.

"You're thinking about it."

Shit, those eyes, taunting him to say something

there'd be no mistaking the meaning of, no taking back. "Possibly."

"I knew it."

It was too soon to kiss her. A nice guy would let her get more than six feet inside the door before backing her up against a wall and stuffing his tongue in her mouth. Maybe find out her last name or offer her a drink. He could do those things—if she stopped looking at him like she *wanted* to be backed up against the wall, swallowing his tongue.

He stepped away and folded her coat over the back of the couch. Caught her hand and made her tag along to the kitchen before they visited the wall.

"Wait," she said, throwing on the brakes. "Is that why you went out last minute to buy a present for Alicia? Because her house was robbed too?"

"Yeah." Thinking about the girl's tears streaming down her cheeks as she and her mother stood in their looted house had his blood boiling again. "No kid deserves to have their Christmas ruined."

Brinn squeezed his hand. "Sorry I gave you such grief at the store. If you'd told me then, I wouldn't have acted the way I did."

Exactly. She would've given him sympathy instead of sexy sarcasm. He likely wouldn't have enjoyed the spark of attraction and hint of jealousy she'd displayed. They probably wouldn't be standing here right now.

"I have no regrets, Brinn." He returned the squeeze

to her soft, warm hand. "Ready to forget about work for the night?"

"Very ready."

"Good." He gave a little tug to get her moving again, and they reached the kitchen in a matter of steps. "I'd tell you to have a seat, but the bastards stole my barstools. Probably would've stolen the breakfast bar if it wasn't built-in."

"No problem, I can lean. Will I be in the way here?"

"Not at all."

"I would've brought wine or something, but all I had in my apartment was soup and crackers."

"The thieves stole all my unopened bottles, but there's some white open in the fridge. That work for you?"

"Direct me to the glasses."

"There should be a couple in the drying rack by the sink." At least the assholes hadn't stolen his dishes. If they'd known the value of his cookware, they just might have. That stuff was worth more than the computer, downstairs TV and other gadgets they'd made off with.

He pulled out a cutting board, chopping knife and the wooden mallet. Next, he retrieved chicken breasts, a hunk of five-year-old cheddar, some ricotta and a bunch of veggies from the fridge, his eyes staying on Brinn as he balanced it all on one arm. Yeah, he was showing off. He'd keep doing it, too, if it meant she continued looking at him the way she was.

She'd changed clothes. Dark jeans molded to her ass and thighs. A low-cut, red top hugged her tits, and accented slim arms. She'd changed her hair too. A wavy ponytail now dangled between her shoulder blades. More casual, head to toe, but no less gorgeous.

Caught staring, he grinned openly. Long eyelashes batted rapidly as she cast her eyes downward, toward the wine, her pale-pink lips smiling while she poured. Lots of contradictions in his date for the night. A dirty mind and plenty of sex appeal. Eating him up with her eyes, then shyly avoiding his stare.

And those lips...hell, they messed with his head. One second she had a fuck-me smile, the next, she could've been a girl who'd never been kissed. All of it seemed natural. Not put on for effect.

The three feet between them was too damn much. So when she extended one arm to pass him a glass, he shook his head. "Not good enough. Come over here." He tapped the spot where she'd been leaning. Once she'd settled in at his elbow, he got to work chopping vegetables. "Want something to nibble on while I prep dinner?"

She wiggled her eyebrows at him. "Depends what you're offering."

"You're worse than a guy." By the smile on her face, she took that as a compliment. "Here. Open up, naughty girl." He slid a long, thin carrot stick over her bottom lip. He expected her to grab it with her teeth, as any normal person would do.

Not Brinn. She looked him in the eye and let him put the whole damn length in her mouth before she closed her lips over the end and started casually chewing.

He believed her when she said she'd never hooked up like this. Didn't mean she lacked seduction skills. His dick was thick with proof of that.

"May I have another?"

"Sure." He pushed a few freshly chopped carrots to the end of the cutting board. "But you have to feed yourself, or we'll be eating these chicken breasts for breakfast. You're very distracting, woman."

"I take that as a compliment."

"As you should," he said, popping one more carrot stick into her mouth.

She giggled as he resumed his chopping duties. Watched intently as he grated the cheese, pounded the chicken.

He focused on not mutilating his fingers—since he hoped to need to them later in the evening—but his peripheral vision served him well. Brinn's eyes stayed glued to his task. The glass of wine she held close to her face didn't succeed in hiding her parted lips. Or the way she watched his fingers, followed the flex of his biceps and shoulders.

Shit, with her looking at him that way, he'd keep swinging the damn mallet all night. These would be the flattest filets in the history of pulverized chicken.

He turned his head enough to make direct eye

contact. He'd known her all of what, an hour, but there was no mistaking the little smile commandeering her lips. "Your mind in the gutter again?" The flush of pink across her cheeks gave her unspoken answer. "Spill it."

"It's pretty dirty."

"I work with a kitchen full of guys, most of them young, all of them hornier than thirty-year-old virgins. The waitresses might as well be naked, they get verbally defiled so much. Pretty sure I can handle whatever pops into your pretty head."

"Wow. I waitressed for years, and I graduated from hospitality management. I can't believe there haven't been complaints or disciplinary actions with that kind of behavior."

"I make sure it stays in the kitchen, and that the waitresses don't hear it."

"That's good." Her head tilted to one side. "Do you take part in it too?"

"Verbally objectifying attractive women? Not frequently, but sometimes."

"Oh. Huh. That surprises me."

Ah, shit. Not good. "I'm no prince." Things would go smoother if she realized that right now. "I work hard, pay my taxes and hold doors for old people. I'm a good guy, not an asshole. And yeah, I enjoy women. Looking at them, having a good time with them. Then I send them home with a smile that'll last all week. I won't guarantee a callback and I don't do serious relationships."

The room got way too quiet.

He pushed the cutting board aside and crossed his arms over his chest. "Sorry if that's not what you were looking for tonight, Brinn. No hard feelings if you want to skip out, before dinner or afterward."

She sipped her wine in what had to be single drops, it took so damn long. She tipped her head for the last mouthful, then tortured him by licking a lingering bead of moisture from her lips with a slow, deliberate sweep of tongue. "Watching you beat your meat is really hot."

What the—?

"You told me to spill it." Her face went from fair to flaming in a matter of seconds.

His kitchen practically echoed, he laughed so loud. "*That* was your dirty thought?" Fuck, she was cute when she blushed. Cute, period. "Babe, stick around awhile and I'll teach you about dirty."

"Okay," she said, shuffling her feet against the gray ceramic tiles.

And now he felt like a dick, warning her off with his don't-get-clingy speech. Regretting it didn't mean he'd apologize for it. He was a decent guy who kept things honest. That was more than a lot of men could claim.

"Your feet sore from work today?" All he needed was the little nod she gave. "Then let's get you off of them." He lifted her by the waist, smiling at her surprised gasp, and deposited her on top of the island that served as his main prep area in the small kitchen.

"Better?" he asked, from his position between her knees.

"Yes." The hands that'd automatically curled around his neck when he picked her up remained there, lightly stroking his skin. "Um, Davis..."

"Yeah?" His dick surged to attention. It liked sexy, feminine voices with that out-of-breath quality. He didn't need a woman to scream or talk dirty—though those were certainly welcome. Hitched breath and soft little moans were just as good.

Which of those would Brinn do when he had her turned-on? When he took her up, up, up and over the edge?

He shifted his weight, bringing them closer together. Denim rubbed denim in all the best places. Even through all the layers, there was no missing the heat radiating between her legs.

"Is it okay if I, um..." Long, dark eyelashes fluttered while she shimmied forward, bringing her denim-covered pussy flush against his groin.

Shit, give him the strength not to thrust while she wiggled side to side. "For the record, I'll say yes to pretty much anything you ask while you're doing that."

Pink lit her cheeks and she tried to squirm backward. *Tried.*

Faster than she could get away, he cupped her hips to hold her in place. "That wasn't a complaint. Ask away."

"May I touch your head?"

A question more people should ask, rather than assuming it'd be okay to buff his shaven scalp with their grimy mitts. "Yeah. Go crazy. Touch anything you want."

With that invitation, her fingers slid over his skin. She traced his jaw, ran the pad of her thumb over his chin, grazing his bottom lip. The lightest touch, but it made his cock hard as steel.

He kept his eyes on hers, even as she looked away to study the details of his face. Her pretty lips turned down as she stroked the scar beside his right eye. Not a frown of disapproval or disgust. Concern, maybe. Definitely something personal. His gut tightened—no, not his gut—the pull was uncomfortably higher, in his chest.

"I bet this was a nasty gash when it happened."

"Yeah, took five stitches to close it up. I used to enjoy a good brawl from time to time when I was younger. Got that one from the corner of a mailbox."

"You were fighting a mailbox?" A small smile returned to her lips. "Who won?"

Cute. "I won. You should've seen the mailbox."

No reply as her fingers smoothed along his eyebrows, moved higher to the top of his head. Front to back at first, then everywhere. Featherlight and so damn good he had to give in and close his eyes.

"Never stop doing that."

"Okay." Minty breath tickled his nose. She caressed every inch of his head, leaning into him until her tits mashed against his chest. "I didn't expect it to be this soft."

"Not what a guy wants to hear when a beautiful woman has her hands on him." The vibrations from her giggle shot straight to his groin. "Believe me, babe, not everything's soft." He could prove it to her—catch one of her hands and guide it lower, between their bodies, curl those delicate fingers over his cock. Not yet. No need to rush, they had all night to enjoy each other.

His rough palms refused to slide easily over the clingy material of her top. He found the bottom edge and slid his hand beneath, holding her close while working his way up her back. "Now *this* is soft."

"Thank you." Barely a whisper, one that became a gasp when he released the hook on her bra. Then a faint moan as his hands traveled to the sides of her warm, silky tits.

"We're doing things out of order here," he said.

"Because we haven't had dinner first?"

So damn cute. "Because I haven't kissed you yet."

"Guess you have two choices, then. You could stop feeling me up and go back to beating your meat..."

He chuckled. "Or?"

"Or you could kiss me."

Chapter Three

BRINN

THANK GOD SHE HADN'T AGREED TO MAKE THE two-hour drive to her parents' house tonight. They'd excused her in advance on the basis of work fatigue and probable crappy weather, but in truth, Brinn had simply wanted to be alone. Not answering questions about jackass Liam or her revised plans for the future. Definitely not receiving sympathetic hugs and pitying looks. Ugh.

After being nonstop pleasant during the Christmas shopping season, she'd been done. More done than her mom's annual overcooked turkey. She hadn't wanted to be around anyone. Until Davis charmed his way into her store, then her evening.

And now, into her bra.

"Your hands are still under my shirt, so where's that kiss?" She'd never been this forward with Liam. None of her previous boyfriends either. It was either Davis, low blood sugar, or the fast glass of wine—maybe a combination of all three—but she felt loose and light-headed. Pleasantly buzzed.

Knowing she'd probably never see Davis again after tonight helped. No need to make a lasting impression. He'd made it abundantly clear he wasn't looking for more, and head office had already promised her a transfer as soon as one came up. Tonight fell into strictly-for-fun land—a place she'd heard about but never visited.

Davis didn't give her the kiss she'd demanded. No surprise there, he clearly liked to be in charge. With his muscles, deep voice and smooth moves, he epitomized the whole "alpha male" thing. They could probably put his sweat in a spritzer bottle and it'd be a bestseller. *Guaranteed to drive a woman into your arms at breakneck speed.* He'd certainly had that effect on her.

Instead of kissing her, his warm lips grazed her collarbone. His mouth moved higher, his tongue making patterns where her shoulder joined her neck, nuzzling behind her ear. She half-moaned, half-sighed, letting her head roll lazily to the opposite shoulder.

"You smell great," he said between kisses, drawing back at her snort to question her with a look.

"Sorry, but all guys say that."

"To you, I'm not surprised."

"Not just to me. It's a guy standard. You all use it and we all know it's a bullshit compliment designed to get into our pants."

"Think it'll work for me?"

"I'm sure it has, many times."

He laughed. Didn't bother denying it. Nor should he, he'd disclosed his status and she'd accepted it.

"What if I told you it's the truth?" he asked. "Would you believe me?"

"I don't know...it's a pretty tired, stock line. You'd have to be *really* convincing." Again with the boldness. Wherever it was coming from, hopefully she could sock some away for future use.

"I'll give it a shot." His nose tickled her neck as he inhaled. "You smell great."

"Oh brother..." Her giggle turned to a startled gasp when he nipped her close to the shoulder.

"I'm all for you saying *my* name. Davis. Whisper it. Scream it. Either's good. 'Oh god' works too. But I'm not sharing you with my asshole brother."

"Ooh, possessive. Almost makes up for the lame 'you smell good' line."

"Yeah?"

"I said almost. Carry on with the convincing."

"With pleasure." Again, he drew a long breath, inadvertently tickling her skin with the tip of his nose. "Are you wearing that perfume you mentioned back at the store? Wait, don't answer." Another nuzzle, this one under her jaw, tipping her head back. "No, definitely not perfume. Something sweeter. Fresher." Instead of moving up to her lips, as she'd anticipated, he headed lower, creating a shivery path that ended at the neckline of her top—in her cleavage. "Here too. So warm and soft."

She tried not to suffocate him by mashing her boobs into his face, but god. "What happened to convincing me I smell good? Warm and soft aren't scents."

"They are for you. When I breathe you in, I imagine how soft your skin will feel when I cover every inch of it with my body. The way you smell makes me think how warm you'd feel, wrapped around me."

Oh wow. Recycled bullshit...quite possibly. But it was quality bullshit with an excellent delivery. And a delivery guy who got hotter by the second. "Okay, I'm convinced."

"Good."

A little shimmy afforded him more space with the girls—an opening he accepted by cupping her breasts and strumming the nipples with his thumbs. Sparks shot from the source, zooming south to where her clit was already engaged in a make-out session with the seam of her jeans and Davis's bulging fly.

But he still hadn't kissed her.

"You can tell a lot about a person by the way they kiss."

"That so?"

She shivered at his words, spoken against her

earlobe. "Definitely. After my most recent loser, I know to be wary of men who put more enthusiasm into washing their car than kissing me."

"He sounds like an idiot."

"He was. Is." She rocked side-to-side, subtly manipulating their position for more friction. If she leaned forward the tiniest bit...

He'd counter by pulling back. Dammit. And he had the nerve to chuckle at her frustrated sigh.

"You can also tell a lot by the way people *don't* kiss."

"You think I'm not going to kiss you, Brinn?"

"It would seem that way."

"Do you have somewhere to be?"

"No."

"Then what's the rush?" At her lack of response, his hands slid from her breasts. They rested on her waist, softly stroking the skin just above her jeans. "Hoping to get over the carwash guy by kissing me?"

For a self-proclaimed player, he sounded kind of offended by the idea she'd use him that way. And wasn't that the most ridiculous, self-centered thing? Laughable, if it wasn't for the whisper of seriousness in his eyes.

"The reason I want you to kiss me has nothing to do with Liam. I got over him the moment I caught him using his dick to massage another woman's tonsils."

Davis winced. A wince could mean he felt sorry for her, or it could mean something even worse.

"And to answer the question that's probably rolling

through your sexy, bald head right now—no, he didn't have to screw around to get his dick sucked. *And*, to answer the *next* question, yes, I'm good at it. Very good, for the record."

Oh god. Oh god, oh god, oh god, she'd just bragged about her blowjob skills. To a strange man. In his house. On Christmas Eve. She slapped both hands over her face. "Tell me I didn't just say all that out loud."

"That your ex-boyfriend deserves a well-placed kick? Or that you give great head?"

"Oh crap." Let her shrink into a teeny-tiny Christmas ball and roll out the front door.

"Brinn." He was smiling. And yes, she was totally peeking through her fingers, but what difference did it make at this point? "Come on, move your hands. No hiding that pretty face." For a strong man, his touch was gentle as he peeled her fingers free.

"What's the alcohol content of that wine?"

"Not enough to make you drunk off one glass."

Seriously, his smile. It was like a drug, relaxing her to a state of looseness she rarely achieved. "Well, so much for that excuse."

He gripped her hips and pulled her forward. The only thing that stopped her from falling off the countertop was his body, wedged tightly between her legs, forcing the rigid seam of her jeans against her clit. The delicious pressure took her dangerously close to the point of no return. She shut her eyes and held her breath, regrouping. Willing her body not to move. Not to have an orgasm *before* he got around to kissing her.

Composure regained—mostly—she opened her eyes. Davis's hazel ones waited. With a naughty grin, he rolled his body, a wave-like motion that made the hard fold of denim rock back and forth across her clit. He'd missed the silent memo about being good, about staying still. Wrong. He knew how bad off she was—it was there, in his eyes. No doubt her ramped-up arousal was written all over her face.

He repeated the maneuver. Then again and again, until she could barely breathe for holding back.

"Fuck, you're sexy. Just let it happen."

God, could she? Should she?

Her hair tumbled to her shoulders, freed of the ponytail with one assertive, male yank. He brought a handful to his face. Inhaled. Smiled like a bad, bad boy. "And babe—you smell great."

"Shut up and kiss me."

His sexy lips twitched, but he didn't speak. The fingers in her hair tightened and he pulled her closer. No more slow, seductive lips teasing their way around her sensitive skin. Just his mouth, taking charge, owning hers as his tongue delved inside, seeking and exploring. She caught it, sucked it hard and deep, the way she'd work his cock as soon as the opportunity presented itself.

He groaned into her mouth. Skated one had down to her ass and forced her even closer, spreading her legs wider as he rocked harder and faster against her clit. That did it. She obeyed him and let it happen, moaning around his tongue, writhing and bucking while she came. Hard. Fast.

Hot and breathless, she slumped in his arms, limper than the boneless chicken at her side. "Pretty sure I'll always remember *that* first kiss."

He chuckled against her hair. "Yeah, me too."

Draped over his shoulder, legs wrapped around his waist, she'd essentially dressed him in a "Brinn" sweater. She *should* move. Free the man. But that'd mean taking her hands off the hard muscles under his t-shirt. Giving up his sensual, masculine scent.

She pressed her nose closer to his neck and took a deep breath. "Hey, Davis…"

"Yeah, babe?" Oh, that sounded good coming from his lips.

"You smell great."

DAVIS

Turning his words back on him—very cute. Having a sense of humor—fantastic. So far, Brinn didn't strike him as a typical female who overthought everything. She also didn't seem the type who routinely went home with random strangers. Not that he had a basis for that. Strictly gut instinct.

Other than the feeling in his gut, Davis knew next to nothing about her. But he liked her. Enough to hope their date took its time unfolding tonight and lasted well into tomorrow. So what if it was Christmas? He had no use for the holiday. He'd hate this year's edition considerably less if he spent it in bed with Brinn.

She planted her hands on his chest and pushed him backward, just enough to slide off the island in front of him. Her pretty blue eyes now had the glassy sheen of satisfaction. And he'd put it there. Before the night was out, he'd put it there again. As many times as possible.

For now, he closed his eyes. Enjoyed her fingers moving over his scalp. A light touch, though not in the timid sense. And not so light that it felt like bugs crawling on his skin. An erotic kind of light. The kind he could get used to, if he wanted the emotional obligations that came with having just one woman's hands on him.

"Feel good?" she asked when he groaned. The two words slid into his ear. Sweet and sexy, like her.

"Yeah. Most of the time, I want to punch people when they touch my head, but your hands feel good. Really good."

"Glad I escaped the want-to-punch list."

He didn't get the chance at a comeback. Brinn stole his ability to string two words together when she slid her hands down his body, unzipping him en route to a kneeling position at his feet.

She stared up at him. Cupped his cock through the boxer briefs. Freed him, then smiled while licking her juicy lips as if she couldn't wait to get a taste.

Fucking hell. Her hand. So tiny and soft. So firm as it tugged him, guided him to that mouth…

"Wait." The single word was all he could choke out. Mentally, he ordered his hips to retreat. The tightness of his clenched butt said the command wasn't getting through. He grabbed the edge of the counter. Had to, or his hands would be on the back of her head, pulling her in.

"Why?" Hot breath teased his cock head—those kissable, incredibly fuckable lips no more than a quarter of an inch away.

"Because I can wait." Four words. He should get a fucking literacy medal for saying more than *ungh* at this point.

"I don't have cold sores or anything, but you can wear a condom if you want to."

"Fuck no, that's not it."

"You just don't want me to suck you?" She pouted, which served to make her lips fuller. "But it's your turn, and I want to do it."

"And I want you to, Brinn, I really fucking want you to, but—" Oh, fuck. Mouth sealing over the tip of his cock. Fuck. So hot. He gritted his teeth. "But not right now."

She stopped, then leaned back on her heels and frowned up at him.

Shit. "I don't want to rush our night together."

"Um, I just dry-humped you on the kitchen counter. And since we haven't even finished prepping dinner yet, I considered that an appetizer, not the main course. Was I wrong?"

"Not at all. But it's different for women."

"Different." She repeated the word as if trying to figure out its meaning, the wheels turning behind her eyes as she stood. "How old are you?"

"Thirty-five."

She patted his chest. "We can wait, no problem. I understand."

"You understand what?"

"Why you need to wait." And now she was tucking him into his boxers—what the hell? "I've dated older guys before. I understand that it takes the body longer to, um...reload. Once you're past the prime years."

Older guy, past his prime? Oh hell, no. "You think I can't get off more than once in a night?" he asked, at which she shrugged. "That's not what I said. Or meant."

"Davis." She brushed her fingers along his jaw. "It's fine. I can wait too. Let's finish making supper and stuff."

He cuffed her wrist as she reached for the cutting board. "This *old guy* doesn't have any trouble reloading."

"Okay."

Like hell it was okay. "I'm not saving up for later."

Another shrug and a cute smirk came his way. Either she didn't believe him, or she was playing with him.

Regardless, he had a point to make. He let go of her hand. Trapped her against the edge of the breakfast bar. "I was trying to be a gentleman. Not an easy thing around you."

Her lips curved into a wicked smile. "Should I apologize?"

"Hell no."

"Good, because I didn't plan to." She snuck one hand into his boxers, coiled it around his cock. "You're still hard."

"You're still fucking hot."

"Still want to wait?" she asked as she milked him with long, tight strokes.

He shook his head and watched her return to her knees.

She took his cock out, surveyed it with lust-filled eyes while rolling his balls in her palm. Her grip on his dick was strong, decisive. He held his breath while she moved in, shaking her head in a way that made her wavy hair brush his bared abdomen and her lips graze his throbbing cock.

She stopped just short of taking him in and looked up. "Sure you want me to do this? Because if the gentleman thing is important to you, *I* can wait."

"I can't." He nudged her lips with his dick. Stopped

breathing when she opened, inviting him inside her mouth. The tip, the next inch, then a couple more, slid between her lips, until his length had disappeared completely. "Fuck, Brinn, you're killing me." Yeah, that was a smile circling his cock. "Your mouth, Jesus, so good. And you're so fucking beautiful."

She said something he couldn't make out. Thank you, maybe? His cock didn't care what the hell her hummed words were, as long as she kept sucking him deep on the down stroke and working his shaft with her fist on the way up. She looked up as she sucked him, eyes wide and loaded with eagerness. Nothing trashy or fake. Enthusiasm, genuine pleasure—or the best impression of those things he'd ever seen.

"Mmm." She let his cock slide almost free of her mouth. "God, you're so hard. So big. I could suck you for hours." Then she gulped him down again.

No mistaking those words, and the desire behind them.

Last for hours? Not a chance in hell. Or heaven. If he managed to hold out for another minute he deserved an award.

Pressure built at the base of his cock. Instinct demanded he close his eyes, hammer into her mouth and come like a fucking geyser. He didn't want to miss a second of her face, those innocently sexy eyes. But watching her pushed him closer. Too close.

"Going to come, babe, you should stop." Jesus, did she just shake her head?

She grabbed his ass with both hands, holding him in place. Her cheeks hollowed from suction. She wasn't stopping.

His balls felt hot and heavy. Ready to explode. Hell, he had two seconds max. "Fuck, Brinn..." Too late. Too fucking amazing to care. He braced his arms on the counter. Pumped his hips. Groaned when her lips sealed around his cock.

Her throat tightened as she swallowed. Then swallowed again, taking everything he gave without hesitation. He ought to bow down and worship at her feet, this goddess of fellatio. All he could manage was a grunt.

"You're welcome, caveman."

That giggle of hers—just, damn. If he could trust his legs not to give out, he'd throw her over her shoulder right now. Show her how much of a caveman he really could be.

She smiled up at him, then scooted out from beneath his frame. Body pressed against his side, she stroked his sated cock. Got it settled back into his boxers even though it would've preferred she continue the petting. She finished with a kiss on the side of his neck. An innocent enough action. Only his mind now knew what those lips were capable of. He'd be thinking about it every time he looked at her mouth. Watching her lips throughout dinner was going to be torture.

"Feed me a nice dinner and you might get another blowjob for dessert."

"You reading my mind?" he asked, tugging her to his chest. He closed his arms around her, bringing them nose-to-nose. "Put it on the breakfast menu. I'm having *you* for dessert."

"Breakfast? I thought you didn't do callbacks."

"I thought salespeople were supposed to be good listeners."

"Are you implying that I'm not?" Her voice rose as she wiggled backward from his embrace.

Damn, she was cute when she got huffy. "I said I don't *guarantee* callbacks, not that I never make them."

"Oh."

"Besides, if you're still here in the morning, no call will be necessary." And yes, he'd officially invited her to spend the night. In his house. Based on a handful of small talk, one smokin' kiss and an insanely hot blowjob. He must be out of his mind.

"Tomorrow's Christmas."

"Right. Keep forgetting that." For reasons other than the handful of presents that'd been stolen from his living room.

She'd provided an escape clause from the overnight offer, so where was the relief that should be hitting him? Maybe that's why he'd suggested she stay—his subconscious thought some warm, friendly company on Christmas Eve would be nice. For a change.

Soft hands cupped his face. Eyes that hid nothing looked straight into his.

Instinct screamed at him to look away. Or put up his

guard, as he'd learned to do early in life. To lock down what she might find if he let her look too deeply. He fought the urge, letting her look her fill, even when his muscles twitched, longing to break free.

Then she smiled, one that lit the whole damn room. "Breakfast sounds great, but just what *does* a girl have to do to get dinner around here?"

Chapter Four

BRINN

BRINN STARED AT HER REFLECTION IN THE mirror over Davis's bathroom sink. Same face, same body. Yet she barely recognized the woman staring back. As if deciding to go for the one-night stand wasn't already in opposition to her goal of finding Mr. Forever. Giving a blowjob to some guy she'd just met—holy crap.

One night of recklessness wouldn't change anything. Tomorrow it'd be back to life as usual. Planning, organizing. Behaving. She'd pull up a chair at her parents' table and cut her serving of dry turkey into appropriately sized pieces. She'd chew with her mouth closed. Have a glass of milk, not wine. Kiss her loved ones on the cheek—yes, with the same mouth she'd used for the blowjob, but never mind that—then she'd go to bed early in her most modest, fuzzy pajamas. Brinn McIntyre, good girl.

That was tomorrow. Tonight she was going with the reckless thing.

Only it didn't feel reckless, and that made no sense. Davis hadn't pulled any punches about tonight. He'd invited her over for a good time—a very good time, if the early events were any indication—but not to start dating.

By all rights, a heavy-duty slutty feeling should've kicked in. She'd certainly had it from doing far less. Like that afternoon at Grand Bend when she'd rolled around on a beach blanket, swapping spit with a sandy-haired bodybuilder from Michigan in full view of hundreds of beach-going strangers. Or the night she'd had one wine cooler more than her tolerable limit and let some guy named Spike—because *that* was his real name, yeah right—get very handsy on the dance floor.

Those times had made her feel like a skanky ho. Having an orgasm on the kitchen counter, sucking Davis's cock before they'd even had dinner...nope, not even a little twinge of regret. Either the stupid relationship with Liam had royally messed up her guy-dar, or Davis was something special.

It was the second option. Only a special kind of man would hunt down a gift for his neighbor's kid after their houses were looted on Christmas Eve. And what guy would try to turn away a blowjob strictly on the grounds of gentlemanliness?

Well, crappity crap. Good thing she knew upfront that Davis was hers for a limited time only. Otherwise, she'd be in for a long, hard fall.

She freshened up and shut off the light in the bathroom. His house looked small from the outside, but there were three more doors off the hallway and a darkened archway down at the end. Access to the back door the thieves had used, probably. The kitchen and living room were open-concept at the front of the bungalow, so the closed doors probably led to bedrooms. One of which Davis slept in. Did his fucking in. And unless something went freakishly off course, she'd be his partner for those activities before the night ended.

Dinner. Movie. *Sex.*

She froze two steps from the kitchen, clutching her stomach as a small riot erupted. Just nerves. Nothing a quick run down the list wouldn't cure. Solid, organized plans solved everything. Well, almost everything.

So. Starting at the top. She had floss and a travel-size toothbrush in her purse. Breath mints if she didn't have a chance to hit the bathroom again before jumping all over him. She'd shaved her legs this morning. Other parts too, so no worries there. Condoms, check. He'd already demonstrated his ability to get her off—hallelujah on that count—and his equipment was above adequate in the size department, but not so huge that she'd require medical attention afterward.

Then came the intangible element with the glowing checkmark—she felt comfortable around Davis. More at ease than she'd ever been with Liam, whom she'd dated for over a year. Based on that fact alone, tonight would be fantastic. Stomach riot quelled.

"Smells amazing," she said, rounding the corner into the kitchen.

"Hey, there you are." He smiled at her while checking the contents of a baking dish in the oven. "Thought you got lost in my mansion."

"I like your house, what I've seen of it so far."

"Yeah?" He pushed the pan back into place and closed the oven door. "Want the full tour while we wait for this to finish up?"

"How much time do we have?" More fluttering in her belly. This time, straight-up anticipation about getting naked in one of those rooms down the hall. Might as well go big since she wasn't going home. She joined him by the stove, slid her palms over the hard wall of abs covered by a snug black t-shirt, then around his waist to his very squeezable butt.

Hint taken. He copied her move—the last part, anyway—and pulled her tight against his body. Either he had a flashlight in his front pocket or he was equally eager to move things down the hall.

How would they do it? Rip each other's clothes off, or take it slow? Lights on, or off? Would he bend her over the bed and fuck her hard from behind, or work his way up her body with a nice detour in the middle before sliding inside her, face-to-face?

He groaned and put a few inches between them.

"No tour until after dinner. If I'm reading those gorgeous eyes of yours correctly, we definitely don't have enough time for me to show you my bedroom." Before she could pout in protest, he yanked her back to his chest. "But we have time for this…" His lips connected with hers. Soft and warm, yet unyielding in their demand.

She melted against him, opening for him as she tilted her head. Full access granted, happily.

His hands slid up her back. Threaded into her hair and cupped the back of her head, holding her exactly where he wanted.

As if she'd want to move with his tongue stroking inside her mouth. Tasting her, teasing her with skills that could—and hopefully would—be applied elsewhere later. God, she wanted that. Even bad oral beat going without, but she'd bet her Christmas commission check that having Davis's face between her legs would end in the best orgasm she'd ever had. His kisses alone made her whole body tingle. His tongue sliding up and down her pussy, swirling around her clit…

"Fuck, Brinn." He broke the kiss but kept their lips close enough to brush while he spoke. "You're making me crazy."

"I'm sorry?"

He chuckled. "You're not, and I sure as hell don't want you to be."

"Good, because I'm really not. I can't remember the last time I enjoyed kissing somebody this much." A dumb thing to say, maybe, but oh well. Being with him loosened her lips in more ways than one.

He reached for one of her hands and inserted it between them, cupping it over the impressive bulge in his jeans. "And I don't think I've ever been this hard from kissing somebody."

"That's...wow." Worth skipping dinner for if she didn't fear passing out from low blood sugar while they were getting busy. "I guess I didn't need to worry about your reloading time after all."

"Saying 'I told you so' isn't nearly as satisfying as proving it to you would be."

Oh, did she want him to prove it. So, so much.

"You keep looking at me that way and I'm going to make you wait a lot longer than the ten minutes until the chicken's done to eat."

Of course her stomach chose this precise moment to make its emptiness—and crankiness at such—known.

He laughed while smacking her ass. "Memo received. Now step out of my greedy reach so I can focus on serving you dinner."

BRINN

Brinn could have licked the plate clean, the meal was that good. If Davis would hurry up and finish his extra-large portion, she'd skip straight to licking the chef instead.

He forked the last bite of chicken into his mouth. God, his mouth. His jaw. His tongue as it swept across his lips, chasing stray crumbs. Chewing wasn't supposed to be sexy. Watching a man eat dinner had never caused heat to gather between her legs, or given her the urge to roll her hips so the seam of her jeans would rub her clit. She'd been on edge since their incredible pre-dinner kiss.

Sitting on opposite ends of the black leather couch, with his legs encasing hers, had *not* helped to settle things down in her southern region. Davis wasn't merely hot, handsome and hunky, he excelled at intelligent conversation. He laughed easily—a sound that zinged through her system, hitting all the important places. He made her laugh too.

Plus, the chef thing. That was so totally hot. She hadn't known him long, but he had "great catch" written all over him. What made a guy like this so averse to being caught?

The fish in question leaned forward and took the plate from her lap, stacked his on top and put them on the floor beside the couch. "Happy stomach?"

"Very. Do you always cook stuff like that for yourself?"

"Not as much as I'd like. Most evenings I'm at the restaurant, cooking for other people. I eat there, and it's good, but not the same as making exactly what I want, and eating it in the peace and quiet of my home." He reached out, caught her chin and stroked his thumb over her bottom lip. "Also, the company tonight sure beats what I'm used to."

The smile in his eyes seemed genuine. With everything he had going for him, though, if he dined alone—anytime or any place—it must be by choice. Much as she wanted to ask him why, he hadn't invited her over to have a heart-to-heart or to be psychoanalyzed.

And she hadn't come over to get attached, something she needed to remember, rather than having these swoony thoughts. "Sounds like we work some similar hours. I pull the noon to nine-thirty shift every Tuesday, Thursday and Friday. I usually grab something in the food court those days. I eat at home the other days, though never this well."

"You don't like to cook?" he asked, letting his fingers slide from her face as he leaned back again.

"Oh, I love the *idea* of cooking. I love food and I'm forever bookmarking recipes and stocking my cupboards with ingredients that I have no real clue what to do with. Seriously, what the heck am I supposed to do with 'cream of tartar'? It's not even cream." She forced her flapping hands back to her lap.

"Anyway, when it comes to the actual process of making the food..."

After a few beats of hanging silence, Davis prompted her by squeezing her legs between his.

"Let's just say I have an affinity for creating Cajun dishes—from every recipe."

"Ah." He winked. "You burn stuff."

"*I* don't burn anything. I just haven't met the oven of my dreams yet."

Dimples, he had them. Not a feature she usually cared for on a man. Too boyish. On Davis, they didn't look the least bit juvenile—in fact, they were panty-melting hot.

He leaned forward and curled his hand over her leg, very high on her thigh. "Cooking is like sex. You don't have to have the best equipment to get great results—it's all about timing and execution."

"If I didn't already know better, I'd think you were putting me on notice that you have a small saucepan, not an oversize stock pot."

He grinned and shook his head. "Come on, naughty girl." He grabbed her hands and hauled her to her feet. "I'm going to teach you how to make dessert."

"Unless it's Oreos and a glass of milk or scooping ice cream into a dish, it's not going to work." The warning fell on deaf ears as he pulled her along behind him. "Seriously, I even fail at instant Jell-O."

He settled her butt against the breakfast bar once again. "How do you blame your oven for the Jell-O?"

Crap. Totally caught on that one. Figured. He'd been teasing her about her flubs since they met in the store.

Inside the cage of his arms, sparks ping-ponged between them. He leaned in and brushed his lips over the shell of her ear. "No Jell-O tonight. No cookies or ice cream either."

She shivered, recalling his earlier words. *I'm having you for dessert.* Now that was a cooking lesson she could get behind. Or in front of. However he wanted to deliver it.

"You're going to make pudding," he said, then backed away, grinning. The jerk, tormenting her with his hard body, soft lips and damn sexy voice.

She tugged at the bottom of her shirt, straightening it when she'd far rather be pulling it off. "The only way I can successfully 'make' pudding is by peeling lids from plastic containers."

His grin stayed firmly in place as he opened cupboards and the refrigerator. One by one, ingredients appeared in a lineup beside her. Milk, eggs, butter, sugar, salt, vanilla, cocoa powder—a fancy kind, not the cheapie, no-name stuff she'd bought the time she attempted to make brownies.

"That's a lot of ingredients. My way of making pudding is easier. Faster too."

One very masculine eyebrow rose over serious, hazel eyes. "That packaged shit isn't pudding."

"Always tastes like pudding to me."

"It won't after tonight. You'll never go back after having homemade."

"You're really going to make me do this?" She sighed in semi-defeat, picked up an unmarked jar and waved it, giving it a double take when the powder didn't budge. "I don't even know what this is—all the white powders look the same to me."

Charming crinkles formed at the corners of his eyes. "They're not. That one's cornstarch."

"Fine." She huffed while returning the cornstarch to the counter. "I hope you enjoy Cajun-style pudding, because I've never successfully made any other kind, not even from a box that says 'just add milk.'"

"There's a first time for everything, babe." He kissed her below her ear, in the shiver zone. "Are you ready for it?"

DAVIS

"What makes you so sure this time will be different?"

Wasn't that a hell of a good question. This time *was* different—for him. He'd had women over for a meal and after-dinner fun, but he'd never offered to share his kitchen with any of them. Not offered, insisted.

Brinn didn't want a cooking lesson, she wanted a

tour of the house that started and ended with his bedroom. Yet here he was, delaying what would undoubtedly be a night of phenomenal sex...to make pudding. Had to be a side effect of the usual Christmas bullshit stress. Nothing more.

He pushed the serious stuff to the back and focused on his incredibly sexy student. "First, you need a big pot."

"Oh, so the size of the equipment *does* matter."

"Sometimes bigger is better, yeah." He grinned while reaching into a lower cupboard.

She giggled as he put a long-handled heavyweight on the counter beside her. Pretty, a dirty mind and a sense of humor. All good.

"This is nice and thick." She slid her fist back and forth along the handle, making his cock throb jealously. "Are you going to show me how to use it?"

"If you stop doing things like that to distract me, yes."

"I make no promises."

"Guess I'll have to keep you busy following my directions."

She pressed her delectable tits against his chest. "Yes, please, master chef—tell me *exactly* what you want me to do."

That list would take all night. His brain was over-flowing with things he wanted to do with Brinn. X-rated things that would make her moan his name. Fun things to make her blush and laugh. Hell, they might still be tackling his list come New Year's Day. A week with Brinn. Not part of his original plan when he'd invited her over, but not the worst idea he'd had. He could do a week without getting too involved. But could she?

Probably not, unfortunately.

Back to tonight. "Measuring cups and spoons are in the drawer beside the fridge. So's the big whisk, a wooden spoon and a rubber spatula."

"Is the wooden spoon for stirring, or for punishment when I screw up your fancy pudding?"

And he'd just mentally added another item to his do-to-Brinn list. He delivered a firm smack to her sexy ass as an interim measure. "Now I'm half tempted to lead you astray during your lesson."

"Only half?"

He groaned when she snuck her hand down the front of his jeans and curled her fingers around his cock. "Sixty percent. And rapidly rising."

"I'll say." She withdrew her hand, winked, then crossed to the other counter, as directed. "Oh wow," she said, as she pulled the chunky silver handle. "Look at your cute drawer dividers." She tossed a cheeky smile over her shoulder. "Are they all like this?" She moved along the counter, opening and closing the short row of drawers and cupboards, getting more of a kick with each one. "I didn't know real people lived this way. I feel like I'm in an Ikea showroom."

"I like things organized." Compartmentalized would be a more accurate word. Sexy times in one box, buddies in another, colleagues in a third, and things that fuck up general happiness—aka, romantic or familial relationships—in an airtight, padlocked safe.

Apparently satisfied with her exploration of his storage solutions, she plunked the requested utensils in front of him, save the one in her hand. That, she twirled between her palms while bending over the end of the prep surface. "You have a very large whisk." Her eyes danced as she surveyed the sturdy, metal wires. "I'm not sure I can handle it."

"Come over here and we'll find out."

She smiled coyly while sliding between him and the countertop. "Here I am."

"Hold on to it while I put our first few ingredients in the pot." He pressed his nose to her neck and his hard-on against her ass. "Then I'll show you how to use it."

"Yes, sir." Her left hand snaked behind her hip, seeking *his* handle.

"Hey, now," he said, though the inch of space he gave so she could better cup him hardly constituted true scolding. "Pay attention to what I'm putting in here." He measured ingredients into the pot. "There's going to be a test on this later."

"Essay style, or multiple choice?"

He curled his hand over hers where it gripped the stalk of the whisk. Guided their mixing motion while speaking softly in her ear, "Multiple for sure. That okay with you, babe?" Might've been his imagination, but her knees seemed to buckle a little.

"Can you give me a sample question?"

He smiled against her hair while reaching for the milk. "Take this and pour some in the pot while I think of one."

"Fine," she said, huffing as she removed her hand from his crotch to follow instructions. "How much?"

"Enough to get things wet." Putting her in charge of the milk left *him* with a free hand, which he slid around her waist. He opened her jeans and skimmed his fingers down, over the front of some tiny panties. Very nice.

"Is that good, is it wet enough?" The carafe hovered over the bowl, shaking as much as her breathy voice.

He slid his questing hand farther between her legs, over the strip of satin. *Wet* satin. "It's perfect." He drew back, enough to delve under the top edge of her panties. "Now add the rest of the milk, but do it slowly, a little at a time." Exactly what he planned to do with his fingers.

She opened her stance for him. He took the invitation and used it well, sliding two fingers along her pussy, stroking with a hell of a lot more patience than his cock would've preferred.

"Jesus, Brinn, you feel so good."

Milk trickled from the metal carafe. Brinn's arm shook where she held it, suspended in the air. Together, they stirred—somehow—though he was damn sure the only communication making it from his brain to the rest of his body right now were the words *get naked* and *fuck*.

71

"God, Davis…"

The sound of his name in her dreamy, lust-filled voice brought him back. Seemed they were thinking the same things. That made drawing the dance out a little longer worth the tight ache in his balls. He circled her clit, eliciting sexy, tortured breathing from his Christmas Eve date. So fucking hot, he could probably ignite a fire with the heat swirling at the base of his cock right now.

"I thought of a question."

"Whatever it is," she said, "my answer is yes."

He chuckled against her neck. "Multiple choice, remember?"

"Mmm…yes."

He did like the sound of that word from her lips. "How do you want me to make you come? A, with my fingers, B, with my tongue, or C, with my cock?"

"D. All of the above."

"So you're perfect." He relinquished touching her to take the carafe from her shaking hand. "Except for the not-cooking thing and your jealous side."

She angled to one side and looked at him, all glassy-eyed and flushed in the cheeks. "Jealous side? Oh…you mean back in the store, because of Alicia."

How could he *not* smile at that admission? But he wouldn't call her on it. No point. "No, babe. Because of my drawer organizers. You want some for yourself."

She wiggled around to face him, eyes gleaming with

naughty intentions. "True, I do want what's inside your drawers."

He stopped her before she popped his button. "And it wants you. A hell of a lot. But you touch me now and I'm done with self-control. I'll bend you over this counter and slide your sexy body through half-made pudding while I fuck you." The scenario had come out of nowhere, but damn. Brinn blinked up at him—once, twice—then tugged his button open.

Things were about to get slippery.

Chapter Five

BRINN

"I'm a man of my word, Brinn."

"I hope so."

A deep growl rumbled near her ear. Then his hands were everywhere, stripping away her clothes with a combination of efficiency and impatience. "Jesus, you're sexy." His gaze moved over her naked body. "Merry Christmas to me."

She'd always worried a little around Liam. He had a serious attraction to sports-mag models, whereas her physique resembled a "before" picture of one of those women. Under Davis's heated stare, Brinn felt like a goddess.

A goddess with more sexual confidence than she'd had in her life. "My turn to unwrap a present." She reached for the bottom of his shirt and tugged it upward.

He helped, peeling the fabric away and tossing it onto the growing pile of castoffs. His jeans followed. Then boxers and socks, leaving him head-to-toe naked and hard all over.

"I've obviously been a very good girl this year, to get a present this size," she said, taking his cock in hand.

Faster than she could give him a come-and-get-some smile, he turned her, bending her over the island—as promised. "Are you really a good girl, Brinn? I need to know."

Her legs shook and her heart raced. "Yes. I'm a good girl."

He leaned over her back, molding his body tightly to hers. "Do you like being a good girl?"

His warm breath on her neck made her shiver. Or maybe it was the question, so loaded with naughty promises.

"No," she whispered. "I don't like it."

"Then I'm going to fuck the good girl right out of you tonight." He knocked her legs farther apart with his knee and entered her with enough fingers and force to make her moan. "I'm going to fill you up, Brinn. So fucking full." He worked his fingers deeper. Teased her anus with the pad of his thumb. "I'm going to make my good girl beg for all kinds of filthy things."

Oh god. Her heart hammered against the cool, smooth countertop. Her pulse pounded in her ears. A dozen dirty thoughts flew through her mind. Things she'd fantasized about, but been afraid to suggest with past boyfriends.

Davis wasn't a boyfriend and never would be. He was strictly a lover. That ought to make him dangerous, yet it made him safe in the ways that counted tonight. She could say anything she wanted without fear of embarrassment or ruining their future. But when she opened her mouth to speak, all that escaped was a needy moan as she arched to meet his touch.

"It's not enough for me either, babe." He withdrew his fingers and took hold of her hips. "I need to be inside you. Deep inside."

"Then keep your word." She reached behind and gripped his cock. "Put me on the naughty list."

He groaned as she stroked. "Jesus, Brinn. I'm on limited control here." He jerked backward. "Hang on, babe, hang on."

She had to give him credit, he took care of the condom business pretty damn fast. Then he was behind her again, this time making good on his word.

"Fuuuck..." he moaned while pushing slowly inside. "You're so tight. Tell me if it's too much."

"God no, keep going." She opened wider, angling her hips to take him deeper. "My loser ex just had a much smaller whisk than yours."

Davis's rhythm faltered as he laughed. "Glad I didn't disappoint."

"Not so far."

Another deep laugh filled the room. "Not anytime

tonight, babe." He thrust again. Not slowly this time. Not gently either.

Air rushed from her lungs. She grabbed for the edge of the countertop, needing purchase under his new rhythm. "Oh, shit," she said as metal and ingredients crashed to the floor.

"Forget them." One hand slid around her body. Two strong fingers pressed against her clit. "Focus on me. This."

As if she could think about anything else with his fingers rubbing hard and fast, pushing her closer to the edge. With his cock stroking in and out of her body, filling her to breathless over and over again. But she still wanted more.

"Touch my ass," she whispered. "Like you did before, but—deeper."

A growl-like sound rumbled behind her. Davis removed his hand from her hip and slid his palm over her skin. His thumb followed the crack of her ass, all the way to his target. "You want my fingers in here, babe? Fucking your sexy ass?"

"Yes." God, yes. A million times yes.

He groaned as he breached her rim. "Fuck, babe, you look so damn sexy, taking my cock and fingers in your hot fucking body."

Heat flared from his touch. A burn she never wanted to end. She arched, pressing backward to meet his thrusts. "Deeper. Harder."

He banded her waist with one arm, holding her

steady while he fucked her, hard and deep. With his cock. With his finger. "You feel so fucking good. Too good. Have to slow down so I last."

She shook her head the best she could. Then reached between their legs and cupped his balls.

"Fuck, don't do that. I'm too close."

Much as she wanted this to go on and on, she wanted him to come. To feel him lose control because of her. So she squeezed. Dragged her nails over the dimpled skin of his sac and smooth surface behind.

"Jesus, fuck..." He thrust once more, groaning as his body molded to hers. "I told you not to do that," he said between choppy breaths. "You didn't come."

"I did earlier."

"Not good enough." He lifted his weight from her back and withdrew from her body.

"I thought it was good," she said, softly.

"Oh, it was better than good." Without warning, he scooped her into his arms, honeymoon style. "But that's still not good enough," he said, kissing her while walking to the sofa.

Her back connected with soft leather as he settled on his knees, with her thighs over his shoulders. "Davis..." She sucked in a breath as his lips coasted over her skin, headed toward her pussy. "You don't have to do this. Really."

"Yeah, I do." His eyes twinkled up at her from between her legs. "I want dessert, but *somebody* wrecked the pudding."

"I warned you I would."

His chuckle vibrated against her sensitive flesh. "So you did. This is better anyway. I'd much rather eat you." One deep, slow glide of his tongue ended the conversation. The next swipe had her wiggling closer.

She slid her fingers over his head, pulling them away just as quickly. "Sorry. Forgot about the punch-zone thing."

He looked up her body, his arousal-darkened eyes meeting her gaze. "You'll never be there. I want your hands on me. Got it?"

She nodded while settling her palms on his shoulders.

Still, he stared up at her. His warm lips and the tip of his tongue teased her pussy, but without purpose. Waiting for her to comply, clearly.

So she did, gliding her hands over his warm, smooth skin.

Back down he went. No teasing now. His tongue moved hard and fast against her clit. He curled his hands over her thighs and pulled her tighter to his face.

"God, that's so good." She cupped the back of his skull and bucked against the exquisite pressure he delivered. The sucking and licking and growling as he feasted on her body.

The switch flipped and over she went. Into that place with flashes of light behind her eyelids. No words. Just hot, rippling, selfish sensation. Davis's tongue. His lips. The endless vibrations. His arms wrapped around her, bearing down, spreading her open and holding her down. *God, god, god yes.*

"I see how it is." His deep, delicious voice floated into her ear.

She cracked one eye open, peering at him from her satiated state. "How what is?"

His handsome face grinned down at her. "You'll do anything to avoid cooking."

"Yup, you've got me all figured out."

"I doubt that's the case, but I've got plenty of time left to uncover more of your secrets." He stole her chance to respond by taking her breath away with a sinful kiss that ended too quickly. "For now, just lie here and give me something sexy to look at while I clean up the kitchen."

She reached for him, catching his forearm before he moved away. "I can help."

"You already did, Brinn. Best Christmas Eve I've had in—" He leaned in and pressed his lips to her forehead. "In a long time."

DAVIS

Much to his relief, Brinn had bypassed the drama category and chosen an action movie for them to watch.

One with lots of ass-kicking. Hot sex too. Like the scene on the screen right now—which had the main characters fucking in the middle of a crowd in China-town. Borderline dubious in the consent department, but Brinn's eyes were glued to the TV. And her mostly naked body was plastered to his side.

The leg she'd slung over his thigh earlier rose. On the screen, the chick was now happily taking a pounding from behind while bent over a newsstand. Beside him, Brinn was rubbing her satin-covered pussy against his leg.

He cupped the back of her leg and pulled her tighter against him. A soft little moan snuck from her parted lips. The speed and pressure on his leg increased, so did the volume of her breathing. Her eyelids fluttered and her hand moved to the front of his boxers.

"Davis..."

Goddamn, that voice. The way she moved, riding his thigh, helping herself to what she needed. So fucking hot.

He trailed his fingers down her back, teased them beneath the edge of her panties. A soft moan filled his ear when he slid two fingers into her heat. "Come for me, babe. Give it to me."

She squeezed his cock through the thin jersey mate-rial while grinding against his leg, hard and fast. "God, Davis, I'm coming..."

Fuck, yeah, she was. And it went on and on. The sensual sound of her panting, the frantic, jerky rubbing as she used his leg to get off. The way her eyes pinched closed and her mouth opened. The flush of red across her fair cheeks. Didn't matter that he'd already come twice tonight. His cock was primed and ready for another round.

"Oh my god." She buried her face against his chest. "That was—"

"Insanely fucking hot."

She peeked up at him through a screen of long, dark eyelashes. How did she do that? Look innocent as a virgin *and* sexy as a porn star?

"You didn't mind?"

"Hell no. What guy in his right mind would mind being your personal sex toy?"

"I could be yours too..." She snuck her hand inside his boxers and stroked his standing-at-attention dick. "How would you like to play with me?"

Oh man. "So many ways, Brinn. So many filthy fucking ways."

She moved quickly, abandoning him on the bed to stand just out of his reach. "Tell me one." She hooked her fingers over the sides of her red panties and wiggled them down a couple inches. "I want to hear the dirtiest thing you want to do to me."

"Let me think."

"No thinking. You already have something in mind —I can see it in your eyes." A little shimmy and those tiny panties eclipsed the curves of her hips. The scrap of red fabric slid down her legs, onto the floor, where she kicked it aside. "If you're too shy to tell me," she dipped one finger between her legs, "then show me instead."

BRINN

"Dangerous request." Davis rose from the bed. He stalked toward her, eyes shining, lips twitching, hard muscles dancing beneath a soft, warm exterior. Like a big, beautiful predatory cat. One who intended to devour her. "You might regret making it."

"Are you trying to scare me?" she asked, when he moved into position behind her.

"No, never. But there's a good chance I will anyway, if I tell you what's going through my head."

"Do you—" God, she hated to think it, let alone say it out loud. As curious and eager as she was, she did have limits. "Does it involve...hurting me?"

"Not if I do it right." His arms banded her waist and one hand slid between her legs to strum her clit. "And I promise to do it right."

"What is *it*?"

He kissed the sweet spot where her neck met her shoulder, chuckling when she leaned backward and pressed her ass against his erection. "Your body already knows."

His words could only mean one thing. This man she'd only known for a few hours wanted to have anal sex. Thank god for the tight hold he had on her, because her knees had turned to jelly.

Davis had already proven he could satisfy her, that her pleasure was paramount. And she wanted to say yes. Her whole body tingled at the thought of Davis fucking her that way. But what if it didn't live up to her fantasies? There was a hell of a difference between a dildo and a flesh-and-blood male. She controlled a dildo. Men controlled—or didn't control—their cocks. She knew that from experience.

"Your heart's racing. I can feel it pounding against my chest."

"I'm just...nervous. I want to say yes, but I haven't had much experience or success with, um, doing it that way."

He turned her within the circle of his arms, bringing them face-to-face. "It's just dirty talk, Brinn. I have no expectations, and I'm not the kind of guy who'd pressure you to do something you're not sure about."

"So you *don't* want to fuck me in the ass?"

He groaned while pulling her tighter to his body. "You're killing me. Yeah, I want to. I'm hard as goddamn steel just thinking about it." He placed a gentle kiss on her forehead. One on the tip of her nose. Another on her lips. "But whether we watch movies all night, or fuck again—in any position—I'm good with it."

Her heart was off to the races. Again. He was a decent guy. A man she could trust with her body. With her pleasure. Somehow, she was sure of it. All she needed was a little courage.

She smoothed her palms over his broad back, smiling when he groaned appreciatively. "You have a great body. I could touch you for hours."

"Please do. Your touch is amazing. Just right."

"I feel the same way about yours."

"Physical compatibility," he said, brushing his lips against the shell of her ear. "We have it."

"I think so too." She hooked her fingers over the waistband of his boxers and tugged them down. "Davis…" A little maneuvering and the barrier separating them disappeared, freeing his sizeable erection. "I don't want to watch movies all night."

"Tell me what you *do* want to do." Between them, his cock pressed insistently against her abdomen.

Every minute of this evening had been incredible. It was about to get even hotter. She slipped from his arms and crawled onto his bed. Goose bumps rose on her arms and her nipples tightened to hard peaks. On hands and knees, she looked over her shoulder and found him staring—a hot, hungry gaze loaded with carnal intentions.

"Turn off the TV and get over here." She stretched forward, head bowed, ass in the air. "I want you to make good on your dirty talk."

In a blink, he'd shut off the TV built into a wall unit

across from his bed. Then he was behind her, stroking her back, her thighs, the curves she'd offered up by assuming this position. Electricity crackled between them, sparking hot every place he touched. He molded his body over her back, brushing her hair aside to kiss her neck. His cock filled the valley of her ass and he rocked his hips, mimicking intercourse.

Every muscle in her body clenched—particularly the ones she'd need to relax in the immediate future. "You're going to use lube, right?"

"You think that's how we're going to do this—just grease and go?" He caught her chin when she shrugged, turning her face toward his. "Any guy who treated you that way deserves to meet my fist."

"You don't have enough hands."

He exhaled, long and low, then rolled onto his back, with his arm covering most of his face.

"I'm sorry."

The arm lifted, revealing intense, hazel eyes that bored into her soul. "No way. Those words shouldn't be leaving your lips. Not with me, and not with any other guy." He reached for her. Repositioned them, spoon style, before she could slink away and find a rock to hide beneath. "You're a beautiful, fun, sexy woman, Brinn. Don't let any man chip away at that with assholish behavior or shitty sexual techniques. When the time and guy are right, the 'lube' question won't even enter your mind."

She groaned and buried her face against the strong-yet-gentle arm holding her close. "God, I'm the worst one-night stand ever. This has to be a first for you, inviting a woman over for sex, but having to give her a pep talk instead."

His chuckle tickled the back of her neck. "You're definitely not the worst one-night stand ever. And everybody needs reassurance from time to time."

"That's what family and girlfriends are for, not the hot guy from the mall whose massive hard-on is wedged between your ass cheeks."

Davis laughed full out this time—with enough force to shake the bed. The sound wrapped around her, a verbal hug to go with the intimacy of his embrace.

Foolishly, she allowed the moment—or more accurately, Davis—to sweep her away. She snuggled closer, warming inside and out when he tightened his hold and kissed her hair. This is exactly what she wanted. A great guy who knew how to make her come. When to cuddle and talk. She didn't get to keep Davis, but he'd proven that quality men existed. She'd go home with the memory of several fantastic orgasms and renewed hope in the male gender. Not a bad Christmas present at all.

Without relinquishing his hold, Davis managed to turn off the bedside lamp and pull the duvet over them. The darkness mingled with the comfort of his body. Exhaustion from the hectic, pre-holiday week hit her hard. Sleep beckoned and she couldn't resist, despite the lure of more orgasms he could undoubtedly deliver.

"Sorry I'm so tired," she said, from the edge of dreamland.

"Stop saying you're sorry."

"Sorry," she said, sleepily giggling against the beefy biceps that'd become her pillow.

A light smack graced the side of her bum. "I ought to put you over my knee for that."

"*Mmm*...I might like it."

"I *know* I would." His hard-on pressed insistently against the spankable area in question. He slid his hand around her hip, settling it between her legs possessively.

Awareness flickered beneath his touch. That's all it was, though—a brief spark. Try as she might, she couldn't find the energy to encourage him. "Davis..."

"Sshh, it's late. I'll still be here in the morning."

"It is your house."

"I meant here," he said, giving her a gentle squeeze.

Maybe she was crazy, falling asleep in his bed. Making herself completely vulnerable to a man she barely knew. Nothing about it felt crazy, though. This bed, the man spooning her protectively, affectionately—everything felt right. Safe.

"Are your eyes closed?" he asked.

"Yes."

"That's good." The lowered volume of his voice made it seem even deeper. "Santa won't come unless you're sleeping."

"Santa's such a pervert."

A chuckle rumbled in his chest. "Half-asleep and you still have a dirty mind. I like it."

She hummed, fatigue finally stripping her of the ability to form words.

"When that right time and guy comes along, I hope he realizes what a lucky bastard he is."

"What?" she whispered. Had he really said those sweet things, or was she already dreaming?

"Nothing, go to sleep. See you in the morning, good girl."

Chapter Six

DAVIS

On the bedside table, Brinn's cell phone started ringing for the third consecutive time. The perky, chirping-birds ringtone had woken Davis on the first go-round. The woman sharing his bed hadn't even flinched at the sound.

He stroked her hair, tucking it behind her ear, making it easier for the little birdies to reach their intended recipient. All she did was smile in her sleep and snuggle closer to him. Okay, not *all*. Her hand also slid down his chest and curled around his cock.

Up and down, she stroked. Her leg wrapped over his hip and her heel spurred him in the butt, urging him closer. "Good morning."

"So you are awake."

"Not completely, but you can help with that, if you want."

"I want." He disentangled, chuckling at her pouty whimper when he rolled away to get a condom. "Here." He snagged her cell and tossed it onto the bed, then tore into the square packet. "Mute that while I do this."

"You don't want to pretend we're getting back to nature?" she asked, giggling while scooping up the phone on its final chirp.

He didn't get a chance to answer, because Brinn had shot upright the second she looked at the phone's screen.

"It was my mom's cell. She's called three times."

"You didn't hear it ringing the first two?"

Early-morning sunshine streaming through the window bounced off Brinn's silky hair as she shook her head. "I woke up when you touched me. I figured it was my parents wanting to say Merry Christmas, but they wouldn't keep calling just to do that, and they wouldn't call from her cell." She looked up at him with wide-open eyes, biting her downturned lip. "I'd better call her back...I'm sorry."

"Hey," he patted just above his knee and winked, "I warned you what would happen if you keep saying that." His attempt at keeping things light and playful earned him a weak smile. "I'm going to grab a shower and give you some privacy," he said, before the apology written all over her face had a chance to slip through her lips. Again. "Join me when you're off the phone. I'll help you clean all those hard-to-reach places."

This time, she smiled for real. "Sounds like an offer I can't refuse."

He left her to her call and headed down the hall to the bathroom. Twenty-eight years old and her parents still called to say *Merry Christmas* at seven in the morning. Hard to wrap his mind around. He couldn't remember a time when he and his parents had exchanged any kind of warm holiday sentiment. Any warmth at all.

He turned on the shower, adjusted the temperature and stepped under the spray. A little cooler than usual, to conserve the hot water for when Brinn joined him. Once he had her curvy, naked body all slick and glistening, he planned to be in here awhile.

When they'd used the last drop of hot water, he'd cook her breakfast. Most women picked at their food and it irked the hell out of him. Not Brinn. She ate with gusto. Watching her thoroughly enjoy the meal he'd prepared last night had made his chest puff out as if he'd received a five-star review at the restaurant. After he'd satisfied her hunger this morning, he'd carry her back to bed to take care of their other appetites.

Then he'd watch her walk out the door. Unless he could convince her to delay her Christmas Day plans. Unlikely, given the way her expressive face lit up when she'd talked about her family during dinner. As much as it boggled his mind, Brinn *wanted* to spend her only day off with her family. She'd probably be there already if the weather had been better last night.

Maybe he'd get lucky and snow squalls would sweep the region before they finished breakfast. A selfish man could hope.

A light knock preceded Brinn's entrance.

"You're kind of overdressed for a shower." He pushed the curtain halfway to one side and motioned her closer. "Wet jeans are a pain in the ass to remove, but I'm up for the job. I might leave the wet t-shirt on you though. Just because."

The dirty-minded woman with a great sense of humor barely cracked a smile. Something was up—other than his cock.

"I have to get going."

"Right now?" At her hasty nod, he shut off the water, wrapped a towel around his waist and stepped out of the stall. "Because of the call?"

"My dad's in the hospital. My mom thinks he had a heart attack."

Talk about the shittiest timing ever. "What's the prognosis?"

"I don't know..." The tip of her nose turned pink, then red, and tears welled in her eyes. "She hasn't heard anything since they rushed him away for tests."

Not a great sign. "Come here," he said, wrapping her in a tight hug. "Doctors do amazing things. No matter what they find, I'm sure they'll have him back on his feet in no time."

"He has to be okay. I'm not ready for him to die."

"He's not going to die." Fuck, what the hell was he doing, telling her that when he knew absolutely zero about the situation or the man's general health.

She swiped tears from her cheeks and looked up at him. "I've got to go. If he needs surgery or—" She shook her head, rather than finish the sentence. "I have to get there as quickly as possible, and it's two hours away."

"You shouldn't drive right now, your whole body is shaking. You're probably in some degree of shock."

"I'll be fine. I need to be there. Just in case."

Yeah, he got it. Worst-case scenario stuff. "I'll go with you. To drive, that's all." Shit. Way to sound like a heartless asshole. Well, he wasn't going to spit out any crap about feelings, so no point in trying to backpedal. "We'll be on the road in five minutes."

"I can't let you do that. It's Christmas Day."

"Like I told you last night, I have no plans today."

"No romantic plans, maybe, but what about your family? I'm sure they're expecting to see you."

He'd listened to her talk about her family last night, but carefully avoided mentioning his own. He no longer gave a fuck about those people, yet Brinn's innocent assumption poked at him as if the wound were fresh and open. "No family obligations. No plans means exactly that—no plans."

"Oh." The softness of her voice said as much as the words she didn't speak.

Sympathy. He didn't want or need it. But he let it slide, because the source was genuine. "Five minutes."

This time, she nodded. "Okay. Thank you."

He returned the gesture and strode from the bathroom. An unexpected road trip with a woman he'd just met, to meet her family under stressful emotional circumstances. Merry fucking Christmas, yet again.

BRINN

Thank god the trip was almost over. The man driving was not the funny, relaxed conversationalist Brinn had spent time with last night. Since closing the Honda's doors, Davis had instructed her to eat some of the food he'd brought. A couple times, he'd asked if she was too warm or cool. He'd acknowledged the directions she'd given. That was the extent of his communication. They certainly wouldn't be sitting side by side in his car right now if he'd acted this way when they first met.

If driving her was such a hardship, why had he insisted? She would never understand men. Never.

"We're almost there. The hospital is just ahead, on the left-hand side."

His response— "K." Not even *okay*, just *K*. Because god forbid he put the effort into that extra syllable.

She'd bitten her tongue so many times over the past two hours, she'd figuratively chewed the thing to the state of ground meat. No point in telling him he was acting like a jerk. Davis had informed her last night that he wasn't a prince. She just hadn't wanted to believe him.

"There it is."

"Got it," he said, indicating a turn that would take them into the parking garage.

"Don't pull in here. Go up a bit and use the patient drop-off area."

He carried on as instructed and found a space to idle near the main entrance. "I'll double back and park, then meet you inside."

"Davis, I appreciate not having to drive while my head was elsewhere, and I had a great time last night, but I'm good from here. I don't need you to hang around."

"I thought you had to work tomorrow." So the broody male had paid attention when they'd talked last night. That made him slightly less of a jerk, but only slightly.

"I do, yes. Assuming my dad's okay, I'll go back to my apartment tonight."

"How?"

"My brother can drive me." Hell, she'd shell out the insane amount it would probably cost for a taxi. Whatever it took.

Davis's forehead creased and his eyebrows drew

together. "That's what you want?"

She nodded and unbuckled her seat belt. This was it. Should she kiss him goodbye? What was the appropriate gesture at this point? Awkward, morning-after-the-one-night-stand crap sucked. "So, um, thanks."

He caught her elbow before she pulled the door handle. "Wait."

Stupid, fluttering heart. Hers was as weak as her dad's, just in a different way. "Yes?"

A hint of smile played across his mouth. "I do like it when you say that word to me." He released her arm and reached behind, into the gap between the front seats. "Here," he said, producing a small red gift bag from the backpack he'd brought along.

"What's this?"

He shrugged, making the muscles beneath his navy-blue t-shirt ripple. "Something I picked up for you."

"Why?"

Warmth lived in the hazel eyes locked with hers. "Same reason I do everything. Because I wanted to. But it'll keep until later." He nodded toward the hospital. "Your dad is top priority."

"Okay, then...thank you."

Once again, he snagged her by the arm, stalling her exit. No talking this time. He leaned in and sealed his mouth to hers. Soft lips. Firm presence. Hint of tongue. The kind of kiss that should be a beginning. A hello. Only it was the opposite.

"Goodbye, Davis," she said, opening the door and stepping onto the snow-dusted concrete.

"Merry Christmas, Brinn."

The *thunk* of the closing door and *toot* from his horn punctuated the crisp December morning. Then he was gone.

Not bad, as endings went. The unexpected gift and sweetly hot kiss totally made up for his stony silence en route. Now she could file Davis under "good times had" instead of "stupid mistakes made."

She filled her lungs with fresh, clean air. Big-city living had many benefits, but air quality wasn't always among them.

The hospital environment didn't smell so great either. Its antiseptic scent invaded her senses the instant she walked into the building, a pungent reminder that she'd entered a place filled with sickness —and death.

She hadn't heard from her family since her brother's text half an hour ago. *Still waiting on test results. No cell service inside. Go to emerg when you get here.*

No news was better than bad news. Still, being in the hospital, knowing that her dad was somewhere within these walls, possibly in rough shape, had her stomach twisted into a knot of epic proportions. Thank god she knew her way around these halls.

Mall and hospital corridors had one thing in common—slow-moving people. She wove around them, gritting her teeth until she turned the final corner toward the emergency department.

"Dad!" Not only did she *not* use an indoor voice appropriate for hospitals, she sprinted down the hall at the sight of him.

He sat on one of the built-in chairs in the corridor. Mom and Zack stood in front of him. All three heads turned at the sound of her voice.

"There you are. Perfect timing. Now we can go home." Mom crammed a bunch of papers into her purse and opened her arms for a hug. "Merry Christmas, honey."

Brinn squeezed her mom, then moved to her dad, hugging him gently after Zack helped him to his feet. "I got here as fast as I could. I was so scared. What happened?"

"Angina. Nothing to worry about," Dad said.

To Brinn's left, Mom clucked her tongue.

"I know angina isn't good news," Brinn said. "But at least it wasn't a heart attack."

"Exactly." Her dad looked past her, to his wife. "Nothing a little rest and some medication can't fix right up."

"Don't think you're going to get away with this dismissive attitude, Joe. When Brinn reads through the information from the doctor, I doubt you'll be seeing such a relieved expression on her face."

Brinn glanced back and forth between her parents. Both appeared pale and tired. Relieved and frustrated as well. Whatever information her mom had, it could wait until they both had their feet up at home.

"Let's hash this out at the house. Give me your keys and I'll go get the car." She extended her hand, palm up. "Is it in the parking garage, or over on the side street?"

"Your dad and I came in an ambulance." Her mom shot another half-worried, half-annoyed look at the patient. "We can go with Zack, or in your car."

"We'll all have to go with Zack. I didn't bring my car."

"Then how did you get here?" Mom glanced at her watch. "And so quickly?"

"I had dinner at a friend's house after work last night, and ended up crashing there. I was pretty upset when I got your call earlier, so I accepted a ride instead of driving myself."

"How kind of your friend, especially with it being Christmas."

"Yes, very," Brinn said.

"You're always working so much, I didn't realize you'd met any new people since moving out there. Is she another store manager from the mall?"

Oh boy. Get the broom and dustpan ready, because there'd be worms all over once she opened this can. "She's a he, and I met him at the mall, but he doesn't work there."

Two blank faces stared at her as the implications of that information set in.

Golden-haired Zack, on the other hand, sprouted a

toothy grin. "Didn't you just break up with Liam a couple of weeks ago, or less?" He laughed when she swatted him. "Look at you, on the rebound. Way to go, baby sister."

"It's not like that, Zack."

"Of course it's not, honey." This time, Mom issued the swat to Zack's arm, silencing him where Brinn's smack had failed. Unfortunately, she then turned her attention on Brinn. "I gather your friend had other Christmas plans—that's why he's not with you now?"

"You know how it is. Christmas is a busy day for everybody." Carefully chosen words. Her cheeks warmed and acid from her churning stomach crawled up her throat, as always happened when she told anything but the whole truth. She swallowed the nastiness down while faking a smile. "And on the subject of Christmas Day, let's get out of here. I need eggnog, stat."

"Me too," her dad piped up.

"Oh, no. There'll be none of that for you." Gwyneth McIntyre linked her arm with her husband's as they started slowly down the corridor. "Unless you want your next visit here to include surgery."

Brinn's chest tightened at the comment. Seeing Dad waiting in the hall had alleviated her fear. Obviously, that had been premature. At least he was upright and mobile. They'd have to work together as a family to ensure he stayed that way. Easier said than done when she lived two hours away.

Zack looped his arm around her shoulders. "You okay, kiddo?" he asked, in a voice low enough that their parents ahead wouldn't hear.

"Mostly. Just worried about Dad. I have to go back tonight, so I'm not going to be much help with whatever needs to be done here."

"Don't sweat it. I'm always around if they need anything."

"Way to make me feel worse instead of better."

Never one to apologize when he jammed his foot in his mouth, Zack laughed instead. "That's on you, Brinn. The only person in this family who thinks you should do more or try harder is you."

He was right. Though Zack, Mom and Dad all had professions in which they excelled, none of them had ever judged her multiple bumbled attempts at establishing a meaningful career.

She'd been top of her class in hospitality management at college, but never properly used her diploma. Because of a guy. She'd worked her way up the store-management ladder, only to have knocked herself down, twice, by asking for transfers. Because of a guy.

Yet her family didn't criticize her choices—job-related or personal—even when *she* could see them for mistakes in the making. They simply supported her. No matter what.

She sighed and Zack squeezed her in response. No more needed to be said on the subject. Especially not on Christmas Day.

"You three wait in the lobby," Zack said, as they approached the main entrance Brinn had used not ten minutes earlier. "I'll go bail my car out of the overpriced parking garage."

"I'll go with you," she said, as their parents continued toward the single row of chairs lining the floor-to-ceiling windows. The walk to the garage would give her time to hit Zack up for a ride later, without raising their parents' interest or concern.

He tugged the lapel of her lightweight jacket. "Walk all that way in this coat that's not really a coat?" He shook his head. "You'd better wait inside too, fashionista."

She opened her mouth to argue, then her jaw fell practically to the ground, rendering her speechless. Zack's step to the left had opened a direct sightline to the lobby area. And the man waiting there.

Davis, twenty feet directly ahead. He sat on one of the lobby chairs, sort of leaning forward. Legs spread, elbows on his knees with his hands clasped loosely in the space between. Even in this environment, he had killer good looks. The shaved head, wide shoulders and well-worn jeans. The strong jaw and hint of a smile. Those piercing eyes, focused solely on her.

Somebody call a custodian, because she'd probably just drooled all over the floor.

"He didn't leave," she whispered.

Zack followed her gaze to the man currently heading her way. "That's your rebound guy?"

For the sake of expediency, she went with "Yes."

"Classy move, waiting around for you. That, or you chose an obsessive stalker type. Scenario one—good on him. Scenario two—I'm gonna kick his ass so hard he has to limp down to the emerg." Good old big-brother Zack, still willing to issue a beat-down in defense of his baby sister.

"No ass kicking required."

Zack's eyes narrowed. "Hope not. I still have to catch up with that last idiot." Meaning Liam. "Or maybe this new guy would like that pleasure."

"Go get the car."

Zack responded to her dismissal with a snort. He nodded at Davis in passing, then cut a straight path to the sliding doors, leaving her alone—relatively speaking —with Davis.

"Hi. You're still here," she said, sounding ridiculously like a breathless, smitten teenage girl. Add a decade to that and it was totally accurate. "Not that I'm complaining."

His smile weakened her knees. Not that she minded that, either.

"Your dad's going home already. That's great news."

"It is. I don't have all the details yet, but apparently it was angina, not a heart attack. Thank goodness."

"Definitely."

"We're going back to my parents' house now. A double celebration today. Would you like to join us? There'll be cranberry sauce from a can, stuffing from a box, and if you're really lucky, instant pudding from a mix."

DAVIS

There it was—the big invitation. One Davis had expected and dreaded since walking into this hospital. Watching Brinn bite her plump bottom lip and sway a little while she hung the offer out there... His answer was instant and automatic.

"Sounds delicious. I'm in." He retrieved his keys, using the opportunity to bury Brinn's cell phone deeper in his coat pocket. He'd secretly transfer it to her bag as soon as a chance presented itself. No point in telling her that was the real reason he'd come back—because her cell had shuffled across the floor of his car when he took the first corner. That information would only embarrass her. Hurt her feelings. He didn't care to do either of those things.

She mimicked his hands-in-pockets stance, using her elbow to motion toward the couple staring this way from the lobby chairs. "Guess you might as well meet my parents now. They're pretty laidback. A little goofy, but good-natured."

"So they're like you."

Her naked lips curved into a smile. "I hope I'm like them, at least in the important ways."

A sentiment Davis had never shared about his parents. Ever. Even as a kid. If they'd invited him for Christmas, he'd have cut them off hard with a "Hell no" followed by a sarcastic laugh.

Today would be like spending time in an alternate reality. An interesting few hours, if nothing else.

"Anything I should know upfront? Topics to avoid, etcetera?" he asked as they walked.

"Nope. They're not like that. Talk about anything you want." A hint of a grimace twisted her lips. "Because they will. Sorry in advance for that."

"Don't be. I can handle anything they throw at me." Growing up in a family of ultra-competitive lawyers had taught him that ability at an early age. Attending law school had perfected it.

"You might not be saying that when they're innocently grilling you about everything you've ever done in your life." Brinn spoke with a warmth and fondness that contradicted the warning she'd issued.

They stopped in front of her seated parents. Brinn swept one arm toward them, and the other toward him. "Davis Rourke, the friend who gave me a ride... Joe and Gwyneth McIntyre, the people who created me."

More dread vanished from Davis's gut. Hard to be stressed after that casual intro. He extended a hand toward her mother first, then shook hands with her father. "Nice to meet you, Mr. and Mrs. McIntyre. Brinn speaks very highly of you both."

Dad stood while pumping Davis's hand. "No formalities in this family. Call us Gwyneth and Joe. And I'm sure we'll be saying the same about you soon enough. Anybody who'd give up their own Christmas Day plans to help a friend in need must be a stand-up guy."

"Happy to be of service to your lovely daughter, sir. Any day of the year." A quick look to his left revealed a blushing Brinn.

Knowing her dirty mind, she'd obviously read into the word "service." As she should have. He'd thoroughly enjoyed *servicing* her last night.

"You'll be joining us at the house after all, Davis?" Gwyneth McIntyre looked a lot like her daughter. Same thick, wavy hair and big, blue eyes. Same engaging smile.

"Only if I won't be intruding."

"Of course not." She squeezed his forearm. Even through his coat, the gesture delivered maternal warmth. "We're glad to have you along."

"Great, thank you."

"There's Zack." Brinn pointed out the windows at a sleek, silver sedan. She waited for her parents to get a few feet ahead, then looked up at Davis. "You should consider this your last chance to bail. Once you're in their house, there's no escaping."

He stepped closer. "Are you going to take me to your

old bedroom and tie me to the bedframe so I don't get away?"

A deeper pink tinted in her cheeks. She slipped her hands inside his open coat and planted them on his chest. "I've never kept a man as a sex slave before, but there's a first time for everything."

Yes, there certainly was. If anybody had told him—even ten minutes ago—that he'd *want* to spend Christmas Day doing family-type things, he would've laughed his ass off. Yet here he was, willingly doing just that.

"Your brother's flagging you." He nodded toward the exit, and the car beyond. "Better go tell him you're riding with me."

"Right. And let him know he doesn't have to kick your ass."

The choked laughter he coughed out had nothing to do with Brinn's light pat on his chest before she turned away. He'd bite his tongue and not insult her brother, but there was no way that guy could kick his ass. Bigger, angrier men had tried. To date, none had succeeded.

Outside, Brinn spoke briefly with her brother. She poked her head into his backseat to say something to her parents, then waved as the three drove away.

"I'm parked in the garage," Davis said, watching her shiver. "Want to wait here while I grab the car?"

"It'll be faster and warmer if I go with you." She hugged herself against the cool breeze that met them head-on as they walked. "Thank you for waiting around for me. If my dad's situation had turned out to be bad news, it would've been nice to have your strong shoulder to cry on."

"I'm glad it didn't come to that, and your dad's going to be okay." Shit. He needed to get her phone back into her bag, immediately. Before it started chirping and gave him away. If she realized he'd hung around to return her dropped cell, he'd go from hero to zero instantly. Not a status he cared to attain. Especially where Brinn was concerned.

Without warning, she broke into a jog. "Gotta go, I'm freezing," she called over her shoulder.

Longer legs enabled him to catch up within seconds. He scooped her hand into his. Together they zigged and zagged through the parking garage, the gift bag he'd given her bumping back and forth between them as they ran.

She reached out and touched his car as it came within reach. "I win."

He sandwiched her between the passenger door and his body. "So do I. And to the victor go the spoils." He snuck one hand under the edge of her jacket and the top beneath. Silky softness welcomed his palm, which he slid upward, to cup her breast inside her bra.

"God, your hand is so cold."

"Deal with it," he said, brushing a kiss against her soft lips.

The tiny taste was all he got. Muffled chirping rose

from the depths of his pocket. Just fucking great. Might as well get this over with. See where things stood once she put two plus two together.

He stuffed his hand into his coat, gripping the offender in a tight fist. "Your phone is—"

"A major cock blocker today, I know. I'll mute it, so you can grope me without interruption."

He cringed as she reached into her jacket pocket. He held his breath, waiting for the inevitable confusion to sink in when she failed to locate the source of the damned chirping.

Out came her hand—and her cell.

What the hell? He opened his fist, letting the phone that was clearly *not* Brinn's sink to the bottom of his pocket. Fuck, whose was it, and how long had it been under the passenger seat? He had a few guesses, none of which painted him in the most complimentary way. And another question—why had he thought the stray phone was Brinn's? Her cell wasn't even the same make as the one in his pocket.

Maybe on some level, he'd known it wasn't her phone. His subconscious at work, giving him an excuse to hang around.

She looked at her screen while flicking a small switch on the side. Instead of tucking the phone away so they could get back to heating up the parking garage, her eyes bugged wide and her bottom lip dropped. "Oh my god, he has *got* to be kidding..." A couple of stabby taps later, she stuffed the device back where it had come from.

"Everything okay?"

"Fine. Just..." She pinched her eyes closed and shook her head. "Ugh, men." Her eyes popped open at his amused grunt. "Stupid jerk-type men. Not you."

"Of course." Good thing he hadn't pulled the mystery phone from his pocket and confessed, or he'd be right alongside the sender of that text. "Want to talk about it, or should we go collect your brother and the two of us will go kick some stupid-jerk ass?"

Some of the clouds cleared from her expressive eyes. "The ass-kicking offer is appealing, I admit, but I can handle Liam. Let's just get going, okay?"

Liam. The ex-boyfriend who'd cheated on her. Whatever the idiot's message said, it had soured her mood instantly. Unacceptable. Especially on Christmas, a day that was important to Brinn.

Davis unlocked and opened the passenger door. He waited for her to get in, gently closed the door, then moved around to the driver's side. Instead of starting the car immediately, he turned to face her. "I don't like seeing you upset."

"I'm not upset. He just got under my skin for a couple minutes. I'm over it." She leaned in, sliding her hand up his thigh, to his cock. Her lips and tongue coasted along the ridge of his jawline, up to his ear. "See? Totally over it."

The soft voice and warm breath against his skin

tempted him. But he couldn't let go of his irritation. "What did Liam want?" Just saying the guy's name raised the hairs on the back of Davis's neck. He shouldn't feel possessive or protective of a woman he'd known less than twenty-four hours. Shouldn't, yet did.

She sighed and flopped back against her seat. "He said he has a gift for me. And he wants to get back together. Says he made a horrible mistake cheating on me and it'll never happen again."

Davis turned the keys in the ignition while issuing her the side eye. "You know that's bullshit, right? People don't change."

"I hope you're wrong about people lacking the ability to change their ways."

"Because you love him and want to take him back?"

Apparently, they'd driven into a black hole, because the car's interior was devoid of sound. He exited the garage and looked over—into the eyes of his thoroughly unimpressed passenger.

"I just had my hand on your crotch, Davis. By choice. *After* reading Liam's text. Not exactly the move I'd make if I wanted to jump at his request to get back together."

Shit.

"Unless you think I'm a slut? Which you might, I suppose, after last night."

And shit again. "I don't think that," he said, pulling onto the street to get out of the way of the car behind them.

Beside him, she folded her arms over her chest. "I'm not sure I believe you."

"You should. I don't lie." Not directly, anyway.

She turned on her seat, leaning into the space between their seats as he drove. "I don't lie either, so here's some truth for you. I rarely have casual sex, but choosing to do so with you doesn't reduce my value as a woman. It doesn't make me less worthy when I'm in a relationship. I don't want Liam back. I wouldn't take him back if he begged me. He broke my trust, and I deserve better. But I made mistakes in that relationship too. *That's* why I hope people can change—because *I* want to change. I'm going to fall in love again. Hopefully next time it'll be more positive and fulfilling, because I learned and grew from my experiences."

He brought the car to a stop curbside and met her in the middle. Face-to-face, practically nose-to-nose. "Hell of a speech."

"I have strong feelings. About pretty much everything." A brief laugh passed over her glistening deep-pink lips.

"I hope that's not one of the things you want to change."

"No."

"Glad to hear it." He slid his hand around her waist and tugged her closer. Brushed a kiss against her irresistible mouth. "Having passion is good."

"It really is," she said, wrapping her arms around his neck and pressing her breasts against his chest.

The action brought his cock to attention. It also brought the gift bag that'd been looped over her arm into view. If he kissed her again, the windows were guaranteed to get foggy, and they'd be significantly late getting to her parents' house. Better to focus on the unopened present.

"You didn't open it," he said, nodding toward the red bag.

Her gaze followed the direction of his gesture. "I haven't had an opportunity. Should I open it now, or wait?"

"Up to you. Open it in front of your parents if you want. I'm sure they've seen fuzzy handcuffs and nipple clamps before."

"Oh god. If they have, I do *not* want to know about it." She freed the bag from her arm, then removed the gold-wrapped gift from inside. "Um, there are *two* presents in here."

"I know. The handcuffs and nipple clamps were sold separately."

Giggling, she tore the paper from the first box. Then made the sweetest feminine gasp. "Oh my god, Davis. You went to the superstore on your way home last night and got the perfume I mentioned?"

"Yeah." He smiled and motioned at the bag. "Open the other one."

"I can't believe you did this." She shook her head, ripping the red wrapping paper from the second box. "The white chocolates too, my favorite kind." Her seat belt clicked and she dove at him, covering him with a full-contact hug and a kiss from her warm, delicious lips. "Thank you, and I love the presents, obviously, but...why?"

"To make sure you got what you wanted, Brinn."

"But you didn't even know me when you bought them."

"I disagree. You made time to help a stranger when few people would have. You had a sense of humor and quick wit. You were pretty and sexy and had a great smile. I knew plenty about you. Maybe it was cocky, but I decided to be the guy who'd make your Christmas wish come true."

"Wow, that *was* cocky. Also very sweet." She placed a soft kiss on his lips, then drew back, giving him one of the smiles that'd hooked him last night in her store. "Just so you know...no gift was required. You already made my Christmas wish come true."

Chapter Seven

BRINN

THE DRIVE FROM THE HOSPITAL TO HER parents' house took ten minutes. Brinn spent most of the time pretending to take in the familiar surroundings of her hometown, but it was just an excuse to repeatedly look at the driver. His handsome profile with its clean-shaven, strong jaw. The way his wide shoulders filled out his dark coat. His relaxed, confident demeanor as he drove with one hand on top of the steering wheel, the other resting on his thigh. Casual as anything.

Meanwhile, her stomach was a mess of intricate knots. First of all—the perfume and chocolates. For a guy who claimed he wasn't a prince, he certainly was charming. How was she supposed to avoid falling for him when he kept doing sweet things? That would require emotional walls she didn't have. A one-night stand with no feelings involved...easier said than done with Davis. He'd already gotten to her.

He might not be aware of that fact. However, they were about to spend several hours in close proximity with her family. The three people she loved most in the world. Also the three who knew her the best.

She'd escaped a barrage of questions back at the hospital because the focus was on her dad. On getting home to enjoy the holiday together. That window had closed, and when the door to the McIntyre house opened...well. It wouldn't take her family long to figure out that she was quite smitten with her new "friend." Then it'd be interrogation time, for sure.

"This one?" Davis asked, indicating the final turn of their journey.

"Yup, this is it. My old stomping grounds."

He whistled while cruising slowly down the quiet residential street. "People in this neighborhood sure do like Christmas decorations."

"You should see the street after dark, when all the lights are on. It's amazing."

He glanced over at her. "You're really into this holiday stuff."

"Why wouldn't I be? *It's the most wonderful time of the year...*" she sang, rocking sideways to bump his shoulder.

His robust laugh filled the car. "Are you always like this?"

"Moderately off-key?"

He looked at her again, smiling and shaking his head. "Adorable. Completely fucking adorable."

Thumpity bumpity, there went her heart again.

"There it is." She pointed toward the only place that'd ever felt like home. "Number forty-seven, that little brick bungalow up on the right."

"Got it." Davis chuckled while pulling into the driveway, behind Zack's car. "How many kids does your brother have?"

"None. He doesn't even have a steady girlfriend. Why do you ask, because he drives an old-man sedan?" She followed Davis's gaze to the six-foot-wide Santa's sleigh on the front yard. "Oh, that. I've looked at it for so many years, I guess it's lost its visual impact."

He looked at her, one eyebrow cocked. "I'm not sure how that's possible."

"You're right," she said, giving her dad's festive masterpiece her full, renewed attention. "I just haven't taken the time to appreciate it the past few years."

Beside her, Davis laughed again. "Guess it's safe to assume your parents really love Christmas. How long have they been putting that thing out?"

"Since I was in eighth grade, so that's...fifteen years."

"Lots of mileage on that sleigh."

"True, but it's still magical."

"I'm going to have to take your word on that one. Christmas stuff doesn't do much for me."

Oh boy. Indifference about the wonder of the season would never do. Especially before walking into her parents' house.

She collected her bag from the floor and opened her door. "Come on, Mr. Scrooge, I've got a story to tell you. Outside. You obviously need a big dose of holiday magic."

"Good luck with that," he said, joining her on the white-blanketed yard. Arms crossed over his chest, he watched her fingers move over the smooth, weathered curves of the painted plywood. He held his position, but his eyes widened some when she used the running board to climb into the sleigh.

"Want to get in?"

He answered with a grunt, though a hint of a smile did tug at the corners of his mouth. "Think I'll pass."

"It'll hold your weight, if you're worried." She slid across the cold bench seat, patting the vacant spot at her side. "If it can hold my dad along with any number of kids, you and I won't break it."

"Still a no. You're flying solo for this ride, babe."

"Where's your sense of adventure?"

One eyebrow rose, and his semi-smile curved into a wholly sexy grin. "I'm not sure that old sleigh can handle the kind of adventure we'd give it if I joined you in there."

Heat flooded her cheeks. Even when she'd had boyfriends in high school, she'd never so much as kissed a boy while sitting in this sleigh. Now her head was full of much more explicit acts. Things that would definitely land her on the naughty list—permanently.

"Save your distractions for later," she said, fanning herself with one hand.

"Will do."

She just bet he would. And she'd love every minute of his distraction techniques, but right now she had some Christmas magic to spread his way.

"So. The story of the magical sleigh. I was thirteen and had recently started babysitting. Not actual babies, just younger kids. Walking them home from school, watching them for a few hours here and there, stuff like that. One of the kids I babysat was a seven-year-old boy who lived down the street. He got cancer. It was very aggressive, and within months of the diagnosis, Tyrone was at home, receiving end-of-life care."

"Shit. I can't imagine."

"It was pretty awful, especially because Christmas was only a couple weeks away. He was determined to see Santa one last time, because he had something really important to ask for. But his health deteriorated really fast. Taking him out to a mall wasn't an option."

"Poor kid."

She nodded. So many years ago, yet she remembered it as if it had all happened yesterday. "My dad built this sled and rented the best Santa suit he could find. He has the physique for the part, as you've seen, so once he got the beard and everything in place, he even had *me* convinced. It was snowing lightly that Christmas Eve, and every single house on the street was lit up with tons of multicolored lights—all for Tyrone. It was the most beautiful sight, like a winter wonderland. The boy's parents wrapped him in a blanket and carried him out to visit Santa in the shiny red sleigh, parked on their front lawn. Tyrone got his wish that night."

Davis had moved closer during the telling, and now stood beside the sleigh, his hands curled over the edge. "That's an incredible thing your dad did."

"A magical thing."

"I can see that, yeah."

She hadn't inspired Davis to spontaneously sing a Christmas song, but she considered the admission a small victory in the spirit-of-the-season department.

"What happened to the little boy?"

"He passed away that evening, in his sleep." She shimmied across the seat, accepting Davis's hand as she stepped down. "My dad has been dressing up as Santa and entertaining the neighborhood kids in this sleigh every year since."

"Do they realize it's Mr. McIntyre in a costume, or do they think he's the real deal?"

"Some of each, I imagine, depending on their age," she said, looking at him as they walked up the path. "I don't think it matters. They always leave smiling, just like Tyrone did." She turned the handle and pushed the front door open, gasping when Davis snagged her around the waist, preventing her from entering.

"You can't go in yet, you forgot something."

She'd left out several details of the story, but Davis had no way of knowing that. She patted her pocket—cell phone where it should be. Keys too. A glance at the ground revealed nothing had escaped from her purse. "Nope, I think I have everything."

Davis caught her beneath the chin and gently tipped her head up. "Mistletoe."

"Actually, it's a ball of plastic holly—"

"Semantics," he said, silencing her with a kiss that made her tingle all the way to the toes she now stood on.

Arms wrapped around his neck, she pressed every possible inch of her body tight against his. Each time their lips meshed, warnings rang in her head. *Casual date, not a relationship. No future. Don't get attached.*

"God, I could get used to that." The whispered comment slipped out as they separated, proving once again that her mouth was synced to her emotions, not her brain.

"I couldn't. I could kiss you a hundred times and never get used to the softness of your lips. The breathy little sounds you make when my tongue touches yours."

Panties—melted. Heart—stolen. "I'm in favor of testing that hypothesis." There, she'd done it. She could barely breathe, but she'd hung it out there, let him know she wanted more time with him.

DAVIS

"Who's letting all the cold air in the house?" Brinn's mother called from somewhere within the house.

The pretty blonde in Davis's arms sighed and pressed her forehead against his chest.

"Are you expecting more company today?" He kept his voice neutral, but inwardly, he cringed. He could handle a few festivity-packed hours with the four members of the McIntyre family. However, if a whack of cousins, grandparents and shit were due for arrival, he might have to manufacture a getaway excuse.

"Nobody else, it's just us. That was code for 'get your butts in here.'"

"Guess we'd better do that."

Brinn muttered something under her breath, then slipped free of their clinch. "Sorry, Mom," she called, while shutting the door. She shrugged out of her jacket and hung it in a small closet, then motioned for him to do the same.

Once the coats were stowed, he followed her deeper into the house. A bungalow, but with a different layout from the one he owned. Bedrooms and a small bathroom at the front here. The center hall ended at the kitchen-dining room combo. Beyond that, they passed through a wide arch leading to a nice-sized living room. Or it might be, if it hadn't been significantly consumed by an enormous Christmas tree. The thing had to be ten feet in diameter at the bottom.

Everywhere he looked, his eyes landed on more decorations. Lights, candles, wreaths, you name it. Nothing too cheesy, but whoa. Sensory overload in progress.

Brinn's brother rose from a chair, hand extended. "Hey. Nice to officially meet you. I'm Zack, the big brother."

"And resident ass-kicker when necessary, I'm told."

Zack snorted while shaking Davis's hand. "Only a couple times. Though I do have one in the queue. Figured I'd swing by the jerk's place and have a chat with him when I'm there helping Brinn clear out of her apartment."

Davis turned toward Brinn, who'd settled on the end of an overstuffed blue sofa. "You're moving?"

She nodded while shooting an annoyed glance at her brother. "Sometime after the holidays. I'm transferring to another store. In a different city."

Well, hell. After the holidays meant January, which was only a week away. "Where are you going?"

"Not sure yet. But my supervisor isn't likely to let me go to another district, so odds are it'll be in her territory, somewhere along the 401-West corridor."

That chunk of geography covered a lot of kilometers. Once she relocated, Brinn might be an hour from his place, or three. Regardless, there was a good possibility he'd never see her again after the move. Unfortunate, because he liked her, and they had great chemistry. But the news also brought relief—for the same reasons.

He'd already taken things further than intended. Being by her side during a potential crisis, joining her family on the most relationship-centric day of the year. Not what he'd signed up for when he'd invited her over last night. He didn't regret doing those things, though. Hell, he was actually in a good mood. On Christmas Day.

He wanted to see her again—he'd decided that when she fell asleep in his arms. But, as she'd informed him back at the parking garage, she wasn't a casual-sex kind of woman. He hadn't needed the clarification. Everything about her screamed "steady girlfriend." He just didn't want one of those, even one as sexy and cute as Brinn.

Knowing they had a predetermined ending changed things.

He snapped out of it when Brinn stood. She smiled at him, skating her fingernails across his midsection as she brushed past. "Make yourself at home. I'm going to help in the kitchen for a little bit."

"Think I'd better tag along for that. I might learn something."

Brinn's laugh drew attention from her mother, currently removing a turkey from the refrigerator. "I love that sound. Wish I got to hear it more often." She plunked the shrink-wrapped bird on the counter and gave her daughter a quick hug and release. "Davis, you go sit and relax with the men. Brinn and I have things covered in here."

"I'm sure that's true. Brinn showed me how skilled she is in the kitchen just last night, at my house." As he'd hoped, a rich blush swept across Brinn's face. Blood rushed to his cock as fast as it had to her cheeks, forcing him to use the old hands-in-the-pockets method of adjustment.

This trick wasn't lost on Brinn. Her gaze dropped, following the movement of his hands beneath the denim. "It's good that Davis isn't in the mood to sit and relax. We can put his expert hands to work for us."

"Expert hands?" Gwyneth's eyebrows rose.

"Very." Brinn smiled and reached for him, tugging at his wrists until his hands popped free, leaving his bulge front and center. "Davis is a chef. Not a line cook, an honest-to-god chef in a swanky restaurant. That's the real reason I invited him along today. Let's put him to work. His meat is delicious."

Oh man. He shook his head at her. The big blue eyes, juicy-lipped smile and blonde curls gave her such an innocent look. But the dirty mind behind her sweet features...damn. First opportunity he got, he'd give her another taste of his meat.

"Well, Davis." Gwyneth wiped her hands on the towel over her shoulder. "You're our guest, and I would never ask a guest to do anything besides have a good time. That said, if you'd like to take control in the kitchen, I'm happy to hand over the reins. And the turkey."

Brinn winked at him. No comment required. He had a damn good idea what was going through her pretty head. And he liked it. Very much.

"I'm happy to do it. Go put your feet up and relax. Brinn and I will take care of the food."

"After the morning I've had, I'll take that offer. Thank you," Gwyneth said, giving him a motherly pat on the arm as she handed off the dishtowel, then left the room.

He moved to the sink and washed up. "Your turn, kitchen wench," he said, snapping Brinn across the ass with the damp dishtowel.

She jumped. Shrieked a little, smiled a lot. But she didn't obey. "First things first. I need eggnog."

He stifled a groan when the top half of her body disappeared behind the refrigerator door, leaving him with a view of her upturned ass.

"Want some?"

Hell, yes, he wanted some. Until she retreated from the fridge with a carton in her hand. "No way. You can't drink that."

"Why not?" She turned the waxed cardboard in her hand until she found the expiry date. "It's good until the end of January."

"*Good.*" He snorted and plucked the carton from her grasp. "High fructose corn syrup. Carrageenan. Artificial flavors and colors. Twenty-one grams of sugar in a half-cup serving. Not good."

"You're a little uptight about food, you know."

"Discriminating, babe." He hated to put the carton of chemicals back in the McIntyres' fridge, but dumping it down the sink—where it belonged—would be kind of ballsy at this point. "You want eggnog? We'll make some. Fresh. You'll never want to drink that artificial crap again."

"I recall a similar statement about pudding. Funny," she said, tapping her chin. "I never did get a bowl…"

He boxed her in place against the counter, leaning in enough to enjoy her soft breasts against his chest—and to ensure she felt his less-than-soft cock pressing against her. "You'll get pudding, Brinn. But we'll finish that lesson in my kitchen, where I can properly take control of my student."

"And if I ruin it again?"

"Then we'll start over. As many times as it takes."

Her eyebrows rose. "That might require more than one night."

"That's my plan."

"It is?"

"Yeah."

"I like that plan." Color rose on her cheeks as she smiled. "Merry Christmas to me."

Fuck, she was adorable. He stole a quick kiss, moving away before the conversation got more specific.

"Let's get to it," he said, grabbing milk and eggs from the refrigerator.

"Wait." She pulled open a drawer, shook out a folded apron and slipped the neckband over his head. "There. That's better."

"For who?" He looked down at the red-and-green abomination.

"For me. And for you." She traced the design on the gaudy apron, paying particular attention to the green patch covering his groin. "Unless you don't want me to kiss you underneath the mistletoe."

A blowjob while wearing a tacky Christmas apron. The image of Brinn's head bobbing beneath the apron had him fully hard. Again. Consider him among the temporarily converted. This really was the most wonderful time of the year.

BRINN

"That was the best turkey dinner I've ever had." Brinn's dad shot his wife an apologetic smile. "Other than the ones you've made, Gwynnie."

Her mom flapped a hand at him. "No need to suck up. McIntyre women aren't known for the culinary skills. We excel in other areas."

Beside her, Davis choked on a mouthful of wine. Brinn did what any Good Samaritan would do—pounded him on the back. Hard.

"Thanks," he said, winking as he squeezed her leg beneath the table. "You really saved me there."

God, could he be any more irresistible? Handsome, sexy, funny, smart. Great in the kitchen, in the bedroom, okay, in pretty much any room. He couldn't possibly be as good as he seemed.

"Does food expertise run in your family, Davis?"

The hand stroking Brinn's thigh froze at her mom's question.

"Only in that they all think they're experts on what's good."

Her family laughed at the perceived joke, and Davis's hand resumed its sensual kneading.

"Then they must've really missed you today, because everything you made was so delicious. I imagine they put you to work in the kitchen at all your family dinners?"

"No. They're not interested in having me cook for them."

"Oh." Her mom must have picked up the same frosty vibe Brinn had, because she straightened in her seat. "Well that's nice too—that they'd rather have your company than your cooking."

"That would be nice."

Would be. From the silence that fell over the table, Brinn wasn't the only one who'd picked up on the word "would" or the simmering resentment in his cool, even tone.

"I apologize." Her mom reached across to pat his hand—the one clenched in a fist beside his wine glass. "It wasn't my intention to pry."

"And it wasn't mine to spoil the mood. It's been awhile since I sat at a family dinner table. Christmas is always sort of a sore reminder."

"I'm so sorry, Davis. If I'd known," she leveled the mom version of a what-the-fuck glare at Brinn, "I wouldn't have mentioned your family."

"No need to be sorry, Gwyneth. They're not dead, they're just lawyers."

Zack being Zack, he laughed. The reaction put a smile on Davis's face, and the mood of the entire table lightened.

"I'll make coffee." Her mom stood and pointed at Zack. "You're on clearing and dishwasher duty."

"I'll take out the trash," her dad said, pushing up from his seat.

"Just to warn you, man, that's code for 'steer clear of the bathroom for the next twenty minutes,'" Zack said, as he collected the dinner plates.

Davis chuckled. "Good to know."

"Brinn, honey, you get the crackers."

"I get the best job," Brinn said, but Davis stalled her with his hand on her knee.

"Crackers for dessert? Didn't I see a pie in the fridge?"

"You did, but it's a store-bought pie. It's afraid to come out with you at the table. It knows it contains *high fructose corn syrup.*" Brinn whispered the words as if they were the devil's work. She tried to keep a straight face, but failed miserably. "I'm kidding. Of course there's pie. The crackers are for popping, not eating."

He narrowed his eyes and shook his head. "Not following."

"Party crackers." She hopped up from the table, retrieved the box of red and gold novelties from the cupboard and plopped them in front of him. "Don't tell me you've never had these."

"Okay, I won't tell you."

The urge to tease him faded as she watched him turn one of the cylinders over in his hand, inspecting it from the ends. What kind of household had he grown up in, that he'd never seen a Christmas cracker? Never experienced the silly, simple joy of pulling the ends and hearing it pop.

She spoke quietly, for his ears only. "See the thin strips attached to the inside of the tube? Make sure you've got a hold of those, then pull it apart. It's going to—"

"Shit," he said at the sharp *crack*.

"Yup. That's what it's going to do. Fun, right? And now you get the stuff inside."

"The stuff?"

"The booty." She pointed at the center portion of the

cracker, sighing when he shrugged. "Your paper crown, prize and fortune."

"You're kidding."

"Wow. You were seriously fun-deprived as a child." She scooped a cracker from the box and tugged the ends, jumping when it cracked, even though she'd known it was coming. "Here's my crown," she said, sliding the purple tissue-paper ring into place on her head. "My prize." She shook the miniature snow globe in front of his face. "And most importantly," she waved the strip of paper, "my fortune. *Your future is ahead of you.*"

"That's deep." Since a wide grin had replaced his straight-lipped expression, her work here was done.

"And totally true." She nudged the toned, muscular forearm that'd distracted her throughout dinner. "Your turn. Let's see what you got."

He extracted the contents of his cracker. The miniature magnifying glass received a dubious look, as did his fortune, which he didn't share. He unfolded the blue tissue-paper crown and put it on his head. "Look good?"

"Very majestic. And totally hot. I'd do you."

"A paper-crown fetish is probably pretty rare, as far as kinks go." He leaned sideways and tucked her hair behind her shoulder, then kissed the spot beneath her ear that made her shiver. "Good thing we both have it."

"Fate at work, once again." She placed a cracker at each of her family's spots, issued a second to Davis, then piled the remaining eight in front of her place. "What?" she asked when he chuckled.

"You're fun, that's all. I like it. I like you."

Just like that, her heart took off at a gallop. Headed straight for the sunset she'd already pictured them riding off into, if a whack of circumstances were different.

She held back the gushiness that so desperately wanted to pour out, knocking off a Davis-ism instead. "Good to know."

The comeback earned her a laugh. And a long look from his warm, twinkling eyes. "You were right about the fun-deprived thing. My parents are both partners in my grandfather's law firm. The dynamic in my house was nothing like what you have with your family. No fun and frivolity, even at Christmas. I can't remember a time when I believed in Santa."

"Oh my god, that's so wrong."

He shrugged. Whatever had prompted him to share this very personal information, he appeared to be shutting it down.

She curled her hand over his and squeezed. A pointless little gesture, maybe, but she did it nonetheless. Touching was a comfort to anybody with emotions. Despite his anti-commitment status—which now made more sense—Davis had repeatedly shown himself to be a guy with depth and feelings. His stupid family didn't deserve him.

"Is that why you don't connect with them anymore,

because you didn't follow in their footsteps and become a lawyer?"

"I did become one."

Her eyes felt as if they'd bugged out of her head. "You're a *lawyer*?"

"Was. Very past tense. I hated every minute. It wasn't amicable when I left."

"But you're happy now, being a chef. It's obviously what you were meant to do."

"Thanks. I think so."

The pumpkin pie arrived at the table, along with her family. Zack first, then her mom with the plates, mugs and coffeepot. Her dad filled the final spot. In his red flannel shirt and with a belly that required reducing to improve his health, he had a definite Santa-ness.

"How many kids did you get this year, Dad?" she asked, shifting the conversation to lighter ground.

"Twenty-three on Christmas Eve. That's two more than last year."

In some neighborhoods, people counted the kids who came trick-or-treating on Halloween. On this street, and more specifically, in this house, they counted the children who visited Santa in his sleigh out front.

"That's a lot of kids," Davis said. "Pretty incredible thing you do, Joe. Brinn told me the story of how it started on our way in earlier."

Across the table, her dad beamed. "I'm awfully proud of my little girl, to be sure."

Her cheeks burned under Davis's inquisitive gaze.

She shoveled a forkful of pie into her mouth and prayed for somebody to change the subject.

"Gwynnie, grab one of the pictures of Brinn in her elf suit off the mantle. I bet Davis didn't see those since he was busy in the kitchen most of the afternoon."

Oh crap. Subject not changing in the right direction.

Davis turned his full attention on her. "You have an elf suit?"

"*Had.*"

The creases at the corners of Davis's eyes sprang into action. "That's unfortunate. I think seeing you dressed as an elf would've ensured my Christmas spirit indefinitely."

Oh god, the way he was looking at her. She could practically read his mind, and it was full of dirty things he'd do to her naughty elf self.

"You know, honey, I still have all your costumes," Mom said as she returned from the living room. "From the first one to the one you wore Christmas of senior year. It's in a garment bag in your closet."

Fate clearly wanted her to dress up as Davis's personal elf. Who was she to argue with fate? "Thanks, Mom. Maybe I'll take it home with me. For old-time's sake."

Zack snort-laughed so hard, he probably passed some pumpkin-pie filling through his nose. "I think you meant, for good-time's sake." Brinn's punch to his shoulder only served to make him laugh louder.

Mom shook her head, rather than referee this round

of sibling button-pushing. "This picture is my favorite. It's from the first year. Brinn with all the friends she gathered to be elves so one little boy's last Christmas wish could come true." Mom propped the framed photo in front of Davis, subjecting him to her walk down memory lane, whether he wanted to take the stroll or not.

Well, Brinn *had* warned him about her family.

"Can you pick her out of the group?" Apparently making him look at the picture wasn't enough. Active participation was required.

Brinn groaned and covered her eyes with her hand—which she proceeded to peek through.

"Yeah, of course." Davis's index finger landed on the mark. "Cutest elf in the bunch."

Her mom patted his shoulder. "That's her. Always shining so bright. Once she got the idea for the sleigh, there was no stopping her. Just dug right in and made it happen. How many thirteen-year-olds would go to such lengths for another person, especially when they had nothing to gain from the effort?"

Davis looked up from the picture. The smile he gave her was like jumper cables on her heart. "Not many."

God. She really should have pulled her mom aside at some point and explained that Davis was not a serious boyfriend. Not a boyfriend at all. Nor would he ever be.

"Excuse me for a minute," she said, escaping to her old room before the crush of reality brought her down in front of everyone. She flopped onto the bed that'd absorbed more boy-induced tears than she had any right to ask of it. If she didn't pull herself together, the poor old mattress would have to deal with a little more renegade saline.

"Hey."

She cracked one eye open enough to see Davis standing in the doorway, hands in his pockets. "Sorry I abandoned you out there," she said, pulling it together as she assumed a cross-legged position. "I just needed a breather."

"Damn. I hoped you were in here putting on the elf costume." He winked. "But it's probably wiser if you wait until we're alone to do that."

"Now I really hope I can still squeeze into it. I'm considerably *curvier*—as you pointed out in my store last night—than I was as a teenager."

"If you haven't figured it out yet, Brinn, I love your curviness." He left his post at the door. The air in the small room charged as he moved closer. Standing in front of her, he trailed his fingers along her jawline and neck, then lower, over the swell of her breasts. "I won't mind at all if you overflow the costume."

"When do you want me to wear it?" she whispered, heart pounding as his fingers ventured downward, inside her bra. The door was wide open. The bathroom was next door, the kitchen only ten seconds away. Yet she made no attempt to stop him.

"Tonight. Tomorrow. The next night. Whenever you're free."

"I'm not free." She bit her lip to stifle a gasp when he rolled her nipple between his fingertips. "But I accept manual, oral and penetrative forms of payment."

"Better keep all those nights open for me. Maybe a bunch more too. With those payment options, I plan on running up a hell of a tab."

"It's a deal." One she couldn't wait to keep.

Chapter Eight

BRINN

OH, THE DIFFERENCE FORTY-EIGHT HOURS made. Hard to believe that just two days ago, she'd been grumpy and frustrated with pretty much every aspect of her life. Fresh out of a shitty relationship that'd stripped her confidence with men to the minimum. So desperate to get the hell away from the Liam wreckage, she'd been willing to shoot herself in the foot, career-wise, yet again. Now everything had changed.

She always hurried through the parking lot to her car. Tonight she had additional spring in her step, extra motivation to hurry home. Only, once safely behind the wheel, she didn't head toward her apartment and the tub of mint-chip ice cream in her freezer. Instead, her car was taking a direct route to Davis's house.

Yes, she was blaming the car. Better that than admitting to following her heart as it galloped toward a man. Again.

This time was different, though. She was in control. Especially now that she had the details about her upcoming transfer. Davis wouldn't break her heart because there wouldn't be an actual breakup at the end of their fling. Just moving day. Then moving on.

No reason she shouldn't fill the remaining time here with as much fun and sex as possible. He had told her to keep tonight—and many more—open for him. She had exactly one month available. Hopefully he'd want to make good use of those thirty days.

Handsomeness and great sex aside, she couldn't wait to talk to him. To tell him her great news.

The mall had closed at five o'clock after being nonstop, wall-to-wall packed with people taking advantage of Boxing Day sales. Given the depleted state of her store's inventory, she hadn't expected to post big numbers today. But she and the two employees scheduled had been run off their feet from the minute they opened the store. Nobody had even had time to check the mid-afternoon numbers.

The end-of-day ring off had come as a very pleasant surprise—they'd not only made their target, they'd achieved a seventy percent increase. *Seventy.* Giddy, she'd fired off a message to her DM. That'd prompted an immediate phone call. Her district manager had congratulated her on the kickass day. Then more.

Brinn's first thought—after *woohoo!*—was that she couldn't wait to tell Davis. Yes, they were extremely new and only casual. So what? He was a nice guy, and he made her feel good. Physically. Emotionally. Who better to share big news with than somebody who made her feel special and important? Nobody, that's who.

A few more turns and she reached his house. His car was gone and the interior was dark, but his exterior light was on, and she could see a note taped to the front door. For her, maybe? When they said goodnight yesterday, his kiss had made it crystal clear he wanted more. If they hadn't both been scheduled for early starts today, she had no doubt they would've spent the night together. They could pick up where they'd left off soon enough.

She parked in his side of the joined driveway and hurried up the front path, not caring that his neighbor watched from the window next door. Alicia's mother, presumably. Brinn didn't blame her for keeping an eye out. She'd be wary of unfamiliar visitors too, if she'd been the victim of a break-in two days ago.

Brinn waved and the woman retreated from view. Okay, not a friendly neighbor. Well, whatever her name was, she could get used to seeing Brinn's car in Davis's driveway. For the next few weeks, anyway.

She stepped onto the low concrete deck and reached for the note, recoiling when she read the first line. Davis hadn't left this note for her—another woman had left it for him.

I want to thank you for being the most thoughtful (and seriously sexy) man ever. Call me when you get home from work. I'll come over and thank you all the ways I know you like, then maybe some new ones we haven't tried yet. See you soon, hot stuff.
—Barb

Bile crept up Brinn's throat. She staggered backward, tripping over her feet and twisting her ankle as she stumbled off the snowy step. Fire streaked up her shin to her knee. She deserved the pain. A suitable punishment for walking around with a ring of cartooned, singing birds above her head. Even when she'd known Davis wasn't interested in a real relationship with her, she'd still pictured them as dating. Some sort of temporary couple. She couldn't pin the blame on a guy this time. The mistake was all hers.

DAVIS

Most people resented working on the holidays. In his five years as a chef, Davis had never asked for any of those days off. First, because he didn't do any of the typical family-togetherness shit. Second, because he loved his job. Third, holiday pay.

He had a bit of cash socked away, but more was always nice. Unlike some chefs, he had no real complaints about his workplace. The owner paid him closer to the high end of the pay scale than the middle, the restaurant had quality management and serving staff, and the place was always busy. All good. The only thing that'd make Davis's job better would be full creative control over the menu.

His boss had implemented some of Davis's ideas. *Some.* Nowhere near all. And that's how things would stay, unless he stepped out and opened his own restaurant. The food part he could do. The people part...not so much. Training up-and-comers who landed in his kitchen—yes. Dishing out reprimands when somebody fucked up in his kitchen—hell yes. That's where his supervisory skill set ended. The thought of managing anything beyond the kitchen walls gave him a headache.

That kind of job belonged to people like Brinn. Listening to her talk about her job yesterday had left him in minor awe. He'd never considered how much organization, determination and leadership it took to run even a small retail store. When he'd spotted her in her store Christmas Eve, he'd mentally labeled her as "pretty blonde salesgirl with a great ass." Hadn't taken him long to realize she was a hell of a lot more.

So that's what he'd do with the extra money he'd earned tonight. Take a certain pretty blonde manager with a great ass, wicked sense of humor, and head full of smarts out on a date. Because now that he'd made up his mind to keep seeing her until she moved, he wanted to see a lot more of her. Soon. Sooner than the old-school date he was planning in his mind. In fact, now would be good.

He pulled into the driveway and made tracks for the house. The wind had picked up since he left nine hours ago, and the gust currently pelting him in the face also rattled a paper somebody had stuck to his door. He flipped up the collar of his coat to block the wind. Then he was on the front deck, pulling the note from the glass while jabbing his key in the cold lock. The steel door opened inward, but he didn't step inside. The message had his full attention.

I want to thank you for being the most thoughtful (and seriously sexy) man ever. Call me when you get home from work. I'll come over and thank you all the ways I know you like, then maybe some new ones we haven't tried yet. See you soon, hot stuff.
—Barb

Davis looked to his left. Barb's lights were on—all of them, by the looks of it. Letting him know she was home. Available.

Right on cue, she appeared at her kitchen window. She gave him the "call me" sign, then unbuttoned her shirt and slipped her hands inside her bra.

He knew from experience what was happening beneath the black fabric. Barb was pinching her nipples, teasing the reddish-brown tips until they were hard enough to cut glass. A quick call and she'd be on his doorstep, then in his bed, giving him anything he wanted from the sexual menu.

That's how they'd rolled for the past three years. Neighbors who occasionally fucked. Somebody convenient to scratch the itch. No strings or expectations, because neither of them wanted a commitment. The kind of setup any guy would envy.

He nodded and headed inside. Stowed his coat on a hook, tossed his keys in the dish on the side table, then dropped onto the couch, feet up and cell in hand. Call time.

Three rings, then it went dead. Not even to voice-mail. Maybe in his hurry to get her on the phone, he'd hit a wrong number. He tapped the digits again, slower and precisely. One ring, two, a third and—

"Hello?"

Yeah. Soft and gentle as he remembered. "Hey. I just got in from work. Were you sleeping?"

"Sort of. Trying to, anyway."

"I know I should say I'm sorry and let you go, but I'm not going to do either of those things." He waited for one of her cute, quick comebacks, but got an earful of silence instead. Maybe he really had caught her on the verge of sleep. "Brinn, you still there?"

"Yes," she said, sighing. "But I'm not good company at the moment, so you'll want to rethink that decision to keep me on the line."

The statement had him bolt upright, feet planted solidly on the floor. "Is it your dad? Do you need a lift down there, because I'm wide awake. I can be at your door in fifteen minutes. Twelve if I hit all the lights green."

"You'd do that? Right now?"

"You have to ask? Of course I would."

"Well, you're off the hook. My dad's doing fine. I appreciate the kind offer, though."

He exhaled and leaned back against the couch, but the tension didn't leave his neck. Something was off. He could tell by her tone. "I didn't offer out of kindness."

More silence.

"Okay, well, whatever the reason, thank you. But I have to work in the morning, so—"

"If it's not your dad, then what is it?"

"What's what?"

"The reason you're in a shitty mood."

"I really don't want to talk about it." Her voice had lost its cool, controlled politeness, these words coming out as a hoarse whisper.

"Then we won't talk about it." He leaned forward, wishing she were across from him, and he could get closer. "Let me come over and make you feel better."

"Why?"

"Because I want to. And you want me to." Seconds ticked by without an answer. Just breathing and the occasional sniffle. "Brinn. One of the things I like about you is the way you say what's on your mind. Give me a clue here, at least. I really suck at the bullshit silence thing."

"Fine." She sighed again. "I can handle a casual relationship where we have sex and I know that's all it is. But I can't be part of a rotation. I guess I'm more old-fashioned that I thought."

"Rotation? I told you I'm not interested in a serious, long-term relationship. To clarify, I'm also not a man-whore with a harem of active sexual partners. If you and I are fucking, Brinn, then you're the only woman I'm fucking." Jesus, did she get hit by double-strength PMS, or was her crazy-chick side finally shining through?

"I stopped by your house earlier. I saw the note on your door."

Questioned answered. No PMS. No crazy. Just standard female jealousy, which usually bugged the shit out of him, but in this case, he understood.

"I saw it too. Then I crumpled it in my fist, came into the house and called you. Not somebody I hooked up with in the past who stuck a booty-call note on my door. You, Brinn."

"Oh."

He snorted. "Hell of an apology you've got there."

"You told me to stop saying I'm sorry, or you'd put me over your knee."

"And *you* told *me* you might like that." He shifted where he sat, opening his legs wider to accommodate his thickening cock.

"Davis?"

"Yeah, babe?"

"I'm sorry for jumping to conclusions."

"Totally understandable. Apology accepted."

"No, really. I'm so sorry. Like, super-duper sorry." Her soft voice and laugh floated through the line. "Sorry, sorry, sorry. I just can't say it enough."

"For a good girl, you sure are misbehaving."

"Sorry?" she said, giggling again.

Yeah, that's the Brinn he'd called to talk to. The woman he'd been thinking about throughout his shift tonight.

"I'm going to enjoy watching you squirm on my lap while I warm your pretty ass with my palm."

Her breath hitched. "What happens after you spank me?"

"I make you come so hard you beg me to stop because you can't take anymore. Then I fuck you, babe. I slide inside your wet, tight pussy and I fuck you nice and deep. I hold your hips and rock into you from behind, so I can enjoy looking at the sexy pink ass I gave you. That's what happens after I spank you." His dick pressed against his zipper, insistent for release and relief.

"Are you on your way yet?" she whispered.

"I am now." He was off the couch and out the door, coat in hand, before he'd even finished the sentence.

BRINN

Despite seeing Davis's car roll to a stop in front of her building, Brinn's stomach leapt into her throat when she heard him knock. She'd been pacing the one-bedroom apartment since inviting him over. To spank her.

She smoothed the lace panties over her hips for the umpteenth time. Heart beating wildly in her chest, she turned the deadbolt, then the door handle. Moment of truth time. She just hoped the truth didn't hurt. Too much.

"Jesus..." Davis didn't walk through the opening. He stood on the other side, hands braced on the frame, his gaze moving up and down her nearly naked body. "How'd you know exactly what I hoped to find you wearing?"

"A bra and panties?"

He shook his head.

"High heels?"

Another shake. The door closed hard behind him, the sound of the lock amplified by the heady silence as he stalked toward her. "White." He circled her wrists and pinned them to the wall above her head. "White. Fucking. Lace."

Oh god, his voice. It was always deep, but right now it was bottom-of-the-ocean deep. Raw in a way she hadn't heard it sound.

"Lucky guess." She arched her back from the wall, pressing her breasts against his chest. The t-shirt he wore was cool from being outside, but the hard body beneath radiated heat. "Or maybe I read your mind."

"Yeah?" The corners of his mouth twitched as his free hand slid inside the front of her panties. "Then tell me what I'm thinking right now."

"That—" She sucked in a sharp breath when he filled her with two fingers.

"That I want to make you come. Right now. That I can't fucking wait. That's what I'm thinking."

"That's what I was going to say." The sound of his low chuckle near her ear made her shiver.

"I'll take that as consent." He withdrew slowly, dragging his fingers up to her clit, which he circled and rubbed until she was rocking against his touch. He lowered his head, captured her mouth. Kissing. Fucking her mouth with his tongue.

The pressure from his hand...god, so good. Warmth swirled low in her abdomen, that sweet, irresistible tugging of *almost there*. "Please," she whispered the plea into his mouth.

His growl rumbled against her lips. Then he gave

her what she needed. More tongue. More friction. Deeper, harder, faster. That perfect amount of *more* that sent her hurtling over the edge.

"God, that, yes *that*..."

"Fuck, babe, so fucking sexy when you come for me." But he didn't stop stroking her, even as her orgasm ebbed. "Again."

She shook her head. Squirmed beneath his touch, shaking from head to toe. "Can't."

He released her wrists, but not to let her go. He cupped her nape hard, tipping her head back, forcing her to meet his eyes. No words needed. His relentless fingers told her what he wanted. What he expected.

Again.

It was too much, too fast, too hard. She couldn't come again. Not so soon, not without a break. She tried to shake her head, to wriggle free.

He refused to allow it, pressing his forehead to hers, piercing her with his silent, hungry gaze.

Again.

God, the pressure, the heat. There, right *there*. So good, so close— "Davis, god, please..."

A string of curses fanned her ear. Then his tongue was in her mouth, taking full ownership as she bucked and panted through the second wave of blinding sensation.

"Wow," she said, as her eyes returned from where they'd rolled back into her head. The first thing that came into focus when she opened them was his neck.

A short row of red welts dotted his smooth skin. Fingernail-shaped welts. From her. "Oh my god, I dug my nails in so hard that I cut you. Was that why you swore in my ear?"

"Totally worth it."

She winced while inspecting the damage. "I'm sorry."

"I'm not." Without warning, he scooped her up and strode the short distance to her bedroom. He sat on the edge of her bed, a wicked-hot smile in place on his handsome face. "But say it again if you want to."

"Sorry?" The question, the word, was out of her mouth before it clicked.

"That's the one." He turned her in his arms, settling her face-down on his lap. One hand spanned her back while the other skimmed over the white lace panties she'd chosen. "So fucking pretty."

Blood rushed to her temples. Oh god, it was happening. He was actually going to spank her.

"You know why I wanted you to wear white lace?"

The large ringlets she'd hurriedly created tumbled around her face when she shook her head.

"Because it's the perfect thing for a good girl to wear." He hooked his fingers over the top edge of the panties and slid them down. "But when my good girl breaks the rules, there are consequences."

His good girl. That alone undid her. Made her desperate for what would come next. Goose bumps rose beneath his touch. On her ass, on the backs of her legs as he pushed the lace farther. If she didn't want this, it was time to speak up. Instead, she lifted her hips, wiggled her now-bare bottom.

He smoothed his palm over every inch of her curves. The weight of his hand disappeared…then landed with a firm *smack*.

She gasped, jerked forward, relaxing as he caressed her tingling skin. The touch ended too soon, replaced by the tickle of air as he lifted his hand.

The next smack rang in her ears. Harder than the first, sending a wave of heat across her backside, and driving her breath out in a *whoosh*.

"Too hard?" he asked, leaning over her back while soothing the sting with a soft touch.

"No, I liked it."

"Good. So did I," he said, delivering the next paddle, and then another.

Each spank pushed her forward, forced her clit to rub hard against his bent knee. Heat flared from the rough contact, bombarding her from both sides. The sting from his hand. The friction from the denim. And it hurt—but god, it hurt so good.

"Fuck, Brinn, the sounds you make. The way you move. *Fuck*." He growled when his hand connected with her ass. No sweet reprieve this time, he squeezed her heated flesh hard, then slid his hand between her legs. A feral groan filled the air as he pushed his fingers inside her needy body. "Makes me so fucking hard whenever I touch you."

She arched to take more, moaning when he moved his fingers inside her. "Fuck me. Fuck me *now*."

He shifted her off his lap and over the edge of the bed. He tucked her hair behind her ear, stretched her arms above her head and pushed her ankles together. "Oh, yeah, right there, just like that. Don't move."

As if she would. Being Davis's sex toy was hotter than hot. However he wanted her, she was in. "Hurry."

"On it, babe." Shirt, jeans, boxers—all hit the floor at light speed. His cock jutted thick and proud from his muscular physique. The simple act of rolling the condom down his length made his biceps and forearms flex. The man was incredible, top to bottom. Inside and out.

Davis stepped behind her, teasing her with the head of his cock while stroking her backside. "Your ass is bright pink."

"Then I hope you like pink."

"Right now, it's my favorite color." He gripped her hips and pushed inside, fast and deep. "Jesus. How do you feel so fucking good?"

"I was thinking the same thing."

He pulled out, groaning as he thrust inside again. "Sorry, but this time is going to be fast."

"No apologizing...unless you want a cute pink butt to match mine."

His rhythm faltered and he laughed—actually laughed—in the middle of fucking her. "This isn't going to work," he said, withdrawing completely.

Before she could sputter out a retraction, Davis shifted her onto her back, covered her with his strong, warm body, and slid home again.

"Yeah, that's better." He smoothed her hair from her face. "Best view ever, right here."

She avoided getting emotional the only way she could—by pulling him down for a kiss. She wrapped her legs around him and tilted her hips.

He answered with another slow, deep thrust. The kind that filled her perfectly. Exquisitely. His tongue swept in and out of her mouth. His hands threaded through her hair. Chest crushed against her breasts, he rocked his hips, moving inside her with controlled intensity. Always connected, worshipping her with every inch of his body. Each strong, deliberate stroke stole her breath, sparked that delicious longing low in her belly. Nudged her closer.

"So sexy," he whispered into her mouth. "So fucking beautiful." He slipped his hand beneath her, lifting her higher, holding her exactly where he wanted her. "Give it to me," he said, his cock hitting that magical, heavenly spot.

Her climax hit hard, forcing her eyes closed, stealing her voice. All she could do was moan and hang on, fingertips curled into his back, heels digging into his butt, as spiraling waves of sensation washed over her.

"Did you come?" she asked after the ability to breathe returned.

His soft chuckle tickled her ear. "Oh yeah. Like rolling thunder."

"Wow, I'm sorry I missed that."

"You were a little distracted at the time."

God, his smile. His eyes. The way he looked at her. Her heart would never survive this *fling* with Davis. The wise thing would be to thank him for the toe-curling orgasms and not see him again. But she'd never been one to make smart choices.

She went for the next best option—keeping things as lighthearted and casual as possible. Let him know she was totally on board with their casual-fucking arrangement. A lie, yes, but she was top salesperson in her district. She just needed to use that skill set with Davis, rather than wearing her heart on her nonexistent sleeve.

She ran her palms over his broad, beautiful back and sighed. "You're really not very considerate, you know."

His eyebrows rose, and creases formed at the corners of his twinkling eyes. "Do tell, so I can improve next time."

"That's the problem—you've already set the bar unrealistically high for the next guy I date. A month from now I'll be living two hours away and going through batteries like crazy because no human male can live up to your sexpertise."

The laugh she'd expected didn't come. Instead, he lifted his weight from her body and rolled to one side—

and not simply to ditch the condom. He looked down at her from his propped position, his eyebrows now drawn together over shuttered eyes. "You got the details about your transfer."

"I did. My district manager gave me the news after we closed."

He responded with silence. And intent staring.

A chill rippled through her. She grabbed the edge of her quilt and pulled it over, covering what she could with the small swath of available fabric. "It's a great position. A promotion, not a lateral move. I'll be managing a million-dollar store in a major mall. That's almost double the volume we sell in my current location. And it's a trainee store, so I'll be expected to recruit and develop assistants to become future store managers. Lots of responsibility and opportunity. Very exciting."

"Sounds like it. Congratulations."

"Thanks." So far, her attempt at light and casual stunk worse than rotten eggs with a glass of sour milk on the side. "So that's why I stopped by your house earlier. I went there straight from the mall, even though I should've known you'd still be at work. I'd just gotten the news and wanted to share it with somebody—" She snapped her mouth shut before the last word snuck out.

"Convenient?"

Special. "Somebody fun, to help me celebrate." She swallowed the gross aftertaste created by the shitty fib.

"Which you certainly just did, so thank you. Multiple thank yous, actually."

"You're welcome." He dropped a superficial kiss on her lips, then pushed up and off the bed.

Piece by piece, her view disappeared. Boxers and jeans went on, then his t-shirt, socks and shoes, until he stood at the end of the bed, fully dressed and clearly ready to hit the road.

"Sorry you had to see that note from Barb. I've told her to leave a phone message or text like the rest of the world does, but she thinks it's more fun to run next door and stick stuff to my house."

Thank god she was lying down, because Davis's bomb would've leveled her. "Barb is your *neighbor*?"

He nodded.

"Which side?" She almost didn't want to hear the answer. Then again, she was pretty sure she didn't need to hear it to know what it'd be.

"Driveway side. She owns the other house that got robbed Christmas Eve. Alicia, the girl I got the present for, is her daughter."

Brinn's stomach churned. She'd waved at that woman earlier. No wonder *Barb* hadn't waved back— she was the competition. Only it wasn't a contest and Davis wasn't the prize, because he didn't do serious or long-term relationships.

Their random meeting had spawned a date intended to be a one-night stand. He'd only spent Christmas Day with her out of kindness. His suggestion they continue seeing each other had come *after* finding out she wouldn't be around long.

Well, shame on her. She'd known all of it upfront, yet she'd still gotten swoony over him. She deserved the vomit inching its way up from her stomach. But she'd be damned if she let him see any of that.

She scooted from the bed, dragging the quilt with her. "I guess you're going home?"

"Probably for the best."

She swallowed the ball of emotions that'd lodged in her throat. Mummified in pastel patchwork, she crossed the room, bumping the doorframe on her way out. Just say goodnight, lock the door and move on—that's all she needed to do. She'd survived worse. This little crack in her heart was nothing.

"I got it," he said, when she fumbled with the apartment's steel door.

"Thanks." Cool air from the triplex's stairwell rushed in as Davis stepped out. "And thank you for tonight. It was really..." *Earthshaking. Intense. Emotional.* "Fun."

"Yeah. That it was." He stroked her cheek, cupped her chin and kissed her. Short, but for real this time. "See you around, Manager Brinn."

She waved through the quilt, waiting until he'd left the building and she'd secured the deadbolt before allowing the useless tears to roll.

DAVIS

The car was colder than the walk-in freezer at work, but Davis didn't start the engine. What the hell was his problem? He'd come over here planning to pleasure Brinn until she couldn't take any more, then ask her out for a nice evening. He'd only accomplished one of those goals. Fuck, had he ever. He'd never been so turned on in his life.

Brinn in white-lace lingerie. The white heels. Her hair done in gorgeous big curls he couldn't wait to run his fingers through. She'd been the picture of sweet and innocent.

Then he'd corrupted her. Thoroughly. He'd controlled every sexy fucking second, made her come so hard he'd thought she might actually pass out. Best sex ever. Incredible woman looking at him as if he were a god among men. And he'd fucked it all up with his dickhead behavior.

He must be the biggest idiot on the planet. She was giving him everything he wanted. Amazing sex. Great company. No long-term commitment. So why had he acted like a jealous D-bag when she mentioned future boyfriends?

He hated jealousy bullshit. Fucking loathed it. Jealousy was the reason he'd ended the couple of serious relationships he'd attempted, and why he'd chosen to avoid that road again. Commitment turned perfectly reasonable-seeming women into raving lunatics. Borderline stalkers. The way he'd just treated Brinn wasn't far off.

He looked up at her apartment windows. No lights on. Shit. Fuck it, he was calling anyway.

She answered on the first ring. "Hi." Not an enthusiastic greeting, but what did he expect? At least she'd picked up.

"I forgot something."

"Oh." Disappointment laced her soft voice. Because of him. "Can it wait until tomorrow? I'm already in bed."

Which is where he should be, tucked in behind her warm, sexy body. "It can't wait, no."

Sheets rustled as she sighed. "Okay. Give me a few minutes to get dressed."

"No need."

"There is for me."

He cringed at the curtness in her quick response. Also his fault. "Not what I meant, Brinn. I don't need to come up, so stay put in your bed."

"I thought you forgot something."

"Yeah, I forgot how to treat you properly. I forgot to apologize when I acted like a dick. I forgot to tell you that I thought about you all day."

For a couple of beats, all he got was silence. Then, "Wow. You're really forgetful."

He laughed, watching the cloud his breath created curl and dissipate. "I'm sorry for being a grade-A jerk. You deserve better."

"You're right." Another soft sigh slid into his ear. "Unfortunately, it's you I want. Not forever. Just until I leave town. I thought you wanted that too."

"I did. I still do." He balanced the cell phone between his head and shoulder so he could rub his frozen hands together. "I don't know why I acted that way, only that I regret it."

"I'd suggest jealousy as motivation, but a guy who doesn't get emotionally attached would never suffer from that affliction." Sweet Brinn wasn't afraid to take aim and fire.

He deserved the shot. "Did I say I don't get emotionally attached?"

"You don't guarantee callbacks. You don't have steady girlfriends. You're not interested in a permanent relationship."

"Not the same thing as emotionally detached." Just the fucking opposite. If Brinn had grown up in his family, she'd understand why he'd chosen to live his life free of heavy relationships.

"I'm really beat, Davis," she said, after a long yawn came through the earpiece of his cell.

"I know. I'm the guy who spanked you."

"My bum is still warm." Her tone had softened, and

though she didn't treat him to one of her adorable giggles, he had a feeling she was lying in her bed, smiling in the darkness. "I liked it even more than I thought I would."

That's all it took for the blood to start flowing below his belt. "You know what to say if you want another one."

No snappy comeback, no flirty banter, just thick silence from her end.

"I want to see you again. That's why I called you tonight, to ask you out. You pick the night. I'll juggle my schedule so I'm free to take you someplace special."

"Special. That's the word I was going to use earlier. I wanted to share my news with somebody special."

And she'd gone straight to *his* house. That ought to freak him out. It didn't. Sitting there in the car, freezing his damn ass off, he puffed his chest out as if she'd pinned a medal on it. Brinn had plenty of special people in her life. Yet she'd sought *him* out first.

"You're going to get hypothermia. If you're not coming back up here, you should at least start the car."

What the—? He leaned forward and peered up, through the windshield. At some point during their conversation, she'd moved to the window. Only her face was visible in the gap she'd created between the curtains.

"Are you still wearing that sexy quilt?" he asked, and she giggled. One of the best sounds ever.

"I left it on the bed. I'm standing here naked, if that influences your decision at all."

"I'm a human icicle. You sure you want me up there? I'm not going to be considerate and keep my frozen hands off you. As soon as you let me in, you're all mine."

Her face disappeared from view, leaving the curtains closed once again. "The door's open. I'll be waiting for you under the sexy quilt."

Forgiveness really was a beautiful thing.

Chapter Nine

BRINN

"Whatever you're high on, can I have some?"

From her position near the upper display shelf at the front of the store, Brinn swiveled to look down at her assistant manager. "Well, I'm high on the stepladder at the moment. Want to trade jobs for a while? I can work on the floor units if you feel like dressing mannequins."

Keeping the store looking full and fresh in the middle of January took some imagination. The effort they put into weekly remerchandising paid off, though. At a time when mall traffic was sparse and most stores in their district were missing sales targets by high double-digit percentages, Brinn's store had a 12.7 percent increase over goal. Nothing record setting, but still on the plus side.

"I'm good down here on solid ground," Lori said. "Besides, I'm enjoying watching you shake your booty to a beat entirely different from the song that's playing. I didn't know people could have such horrible rhythm in real life—I thought that was something you only saw on sitcoms."

"I have rhythm when it counts, just so you know."

"Ooh, finally, some dirty details about the new mystery man." Lori rubbed her hands together. "About time you spilled the boinking beans."

She turned her back on Lori under the guise of continuing with changing the front display. One of these days, she really needed to work on her poker face. "What makes you think I was talking about now? I never said anything about a new guy or any sort of *boinking*, rhythmic or otherwise."

Lori had one of those unique, husky-in-a-phone-sex-way voices, and a laugh to match. Right now, that laugh rang loud enough to drown out head office's selected upbeat tunes of the month.

"You've had a perma-smile on your face since eight a.m. Boxing Day. *Nobody* in retail smiles then. Or at this time of year. I know you're excited about your promotion, but this is different. You have the glow of a well-boinked woman. And frankly, there are days when you smell like sex."

Brinn jerked around, grabbing the edge of the shelf to keep her balance, and sending a headless, naked torso flying in the process. "But I always shower before work. Oh my god, what if Carol smelled it on me when she was here last week?"

"Aha!" Thank god the mall was a ghost town, because Lori's jumping and screaming weren't a terribly professional display of behavior. "I knew it. Who is he, where'd you meet him? How often are you getting it on? Does he know you're leaving in two weeks?"

"You tricked me? You're horrible, you know that? I'm going to leave a note for your next manager, telling her you'd benefit from a thorough refresher of *all* the management-trainee manuals."

"That's pure evil. I'll fall into a boredom-induced coma if I have to go through all those manuals again."

Brinn shrugged after descending the ladder. "Don't let my sweet-and-innocent exterior fool you," she said in mock warning, while bending over to search for the fallen dummy. "There's a calculating, highly inventive bad girl hiding behind my pink lip gloss and high ponytail."

Lori didn't answer. Well, crap. Maybe Brinn's joke sucked as much as her dancing and cooking. "Hey," she said, while pulling the slightly worse for wear mannequin from beneath a rolling rack of yoga pants. "You knew I was kidding about the retraining, right?" Still nothing. "Lori?" she asked, turning as she emerged from the black and gray spandex.

Lori met her with a smile. One that said, *Oh yeah, you are sooo telling me all about this guy when he leaves*, as she tilted her head in Davis's direction. "This gentleman would like to speak with you."

Gentleman indeed. Davis stood next to Brinn's assistant manager sporting a fresh shave, a black suit jacket with crisp white shirt beneath, and a smile hot enough to take the chill off even the coldest winter day. Thank goodness she wasn't up on the ladder, she'd have fallen for sure. Oh, who was she kidding? She'd long since *fallen* for Davis Rourke.

"Hi," she said, after silently commanding her rioting libido to stand down. Good grief, her sex drive was out of control. They'd had sex this morning. Long, hot, delicious midmorning sex. He'd already made her come three times today. Twice with his mouth and once while he fucked her. She ought to be satiated, at least until later tonight. But seeing him dressed like this...lordy.

"Sorry for intruding on your workday." The bottom of his jacket parted below the buttons when he slid his hands into the front pockets of his jeans, a posture that made him impossibly hotter. "I texted you a few times, but you didn't answer."

From several feet away, Lori snorted. "That's because her phone's in the stockroom. Brinn doesn't allow cell phones out front. She looks young and hip, but I think she's actually a fifty-year-old hard-ass in disguise."

"You're fired," Brinn said, then stuck her tongue out. "There. Is that juvenile enough for you?"

"It's a start." Lori placed a neatly folded sweater on

top of the floor unit she'd been merchandising. "I'm going to take five and grab a bottle of water." Lori took the long way around the racks, making a pit stop beside Davis, rather than walk straight out the door. "She won't let us have any beverages other than water out front, either. Is she as bossy with you as she is with her employees?"

"Oh yeah. Totally demanding." A mischievous twinkle shone in the hazel eyes locked with hers. He didn't need to say more. He was referencing sex and she knew it.

Fuck me now. Give me more. Put your finger in my ass. Make me come. She'd demanded those things, and more, to Davis. And he'd been happy to oblige.

"Okay, then. Maybe I'll take the long way to the food court." Lori saluted, then made a beeline for the door.

As soon as Brinn was alone in the store with him, the space seemed to shrink. She'd had the same sensation the first and only other time he'd been in here with her—afterhours on Christmas Eve. He'd looked sexy and handsome that night. Charming but a little bit dangerous.

The man standing in front of her now put that guy to shame. Because she'd learned so much about him in the weeks since their first spontaneous encounter. When she looked at him now, she saw the man he was inside. His warmth and passion. His sense of humor and empathy. However, his exterior at the moment definitely added to the package.

"Are you moonlighting as a male model or some-thing? I haven't seen you wear a suit to the restaurant." And since she'd spent almost every available moment with him for the past two-plus weeks, she'd seen him dress for work—and had *undressed* him after work—plenty of times.

"It's only half a suit." He glanced down at the jacket. "That's why I stopped by, to get your opinion on the clothes before heading to a meeting with the owner."

Stupid as it was, her heart picked up a couple beats. She couldn't help it, everything about this moment screamed *relationship,* and not just the temporary, *he's only in it for the hot sex* kind.

She stepped within touching distance and smoothed her hands over his lapels. "My opinion is that whatever you ask for in that meeting, the answer will be yes. Especially if the owner is a woman."

"Is that what your answer will be later, if I show up at your apartment wearing this?" He hadn't removed his hands from his pockets, yet she could feel his touch—everywhere.

"That'll be my answer no matter what you're wear-ing. Or asking." Hormones and chemistry told her to lean in, go to her toes and see how deliciously warm his sexy, smiling lips were. Professionalism and good old-fashioned common sense persevered. She exhaled, gently shaking off the buzz being close to Davis always initiated. "Sorry, I got sidetracked by your hotness."

"No complaints from this guy. I like the track you were on."

"Me too, but that's not why you braved the busy mall on your way to work," she said, making a sweeping gesture toward the front of the store.

Davis looked over his shoulder at the near-empty corridor. "Don't let this deadsville place get you down, babe. That mall you're transferring to makes this one look like a mom-and-pop show. Your new store has twice the square footage you've got here. You're going to do amazing things there."

She nodded, but the lump that'd formed in her throat prevented properly answering. Since they'd both had Wednesday off, Davis had gone with her to check out the new location. He'd even helped her scout out an apartment. That endeavor had taken the majority of the day. Together they'd exhausted the classifieds and driven the unknown streets, viewing one unsuitable unit after another, until they randomly stumbled upon a place that would work. It was small and a bit of a hike from the mall, but it was clean, cheap and available immediately. Other than being two hours away from Davis, it was a winner.

She cleared her throat and focused on the present. The handsome man in front of her. The suit. "So, tell me what kind of opinion you need, aside from confirmation that you're insanely hot."

"Hold that thought for later," he said, winking. "The truth is, you've inspired me. The way you're focused on your career, your willingness to make big changes and do whatever it takes to get ahead. You're not content with the status quo, despite being really good at it."

"Wow, you make me sound like queen of the go-getters."

"You are in my eyes."

If he only knew the truth. The promotion was lucky timing. She'd requested a transfer—even if it meant taking a lesser position—strictly as a means to run away from another screw-up in her personal life. A cowardly move, not a bold one.

"You wanted and deserved more, so you asked for it," he continued. "And it paid off. I decided to take a page out of your book and set up a meeting with the owner and general manager. I'm going to ask for creative control over the menu. At least a hell of a lot more than I've had to this point. I've got a ton of great ideas. Every high-end steakhouse offers essentially the same options. The stuff I'm proposing will break us out of that same-old, same-old rut."

"Wow...you sold me."

"Thanks. That helps take the edge off my nerves."

"Nerves? What nerves? You're dressed for success, have a great plan and pitch, and when you talk about food, it's with absolute passion." To hell with professionalism, for once. She planted her hands on his chest, rose to her toes and kissed him. "For luck, though I know you won't need it."

"I hope you're right." He pulled his hands from

his pockets and flicked the black lapels of his tailored-to-perfection jacket. "And this is okay for that kind of meeting? I thought a two-piece suit might be over the top. Then I didn't know if I should wear a tie, or go without, since I wasn't wearing the suit pants." He swiped one palm over his head, down the back of his neck, which he massaged with rough-looking pinches. "Food is my thing, not fashion. I should've asked you before you left for work, but I was hoping to surprise you with some good news of my own later."

God, she loved this man.

"Hey, you okay?" He gripped her elbow when she took a dizzy step backward. "Did you bring the lunch stuff I set out for you? Maybe you should take a break and get something to eat."

Every word out of his mouth, every caring action, made the realization worse. She hadn't just gotten addicted to the sex, or a little emotionally attached. She'd fallen *in love* with Davis. Madly. Completely.

She nodded and rallied some steel for her spine. "That's probably a good idea. I'll go on break soon."

"Good. Do that." He rubbed circles over her forearm with his thumb, his narrowed eyes fixed intently on her face. "You're probably suffering from fatigue too. I've been depriving you of too much sleep. You should stop waiting up for me every night."

If they had any amount of future, that'd be a prac-tical point. With only a limited number of nights together left, wasting them on sleep wasn't an option that crossed her mind for a single moment.

"I'm sure it's just low blood sugar. I'll take time to eat when Lori comes back, I promise." As if cued, her assistant came around the corner, and twenty seconds later, walked into the store. "Speak of the devil." Brinn freed her arm from his protective touch and put space between them. "What time is your meeting?"

Davis flipped the edge of his sleeve up to check his watch. "Shit. I'm not late, but I've got to move it."

"Get going," she said, shooing him with her finger-tips. "Impress the hell out of them."

Halfway out of the store, he turned back and pointed at Lori. "Make sure the manager goes on a break and eats soon."

"Will do," Lori said, issuing a salute.

"Let me know how it went," Brinn called before he got underway again. "I'll still be awake when you finish your shift."

"Noted."

"Whoa." Lori fanned herself after Davis and his killer smile disappeared from sight. "That man is a serious upgrade from your last boyfriend."

"I know. He's got a great job that he cares about, he makes me laugh all the time, and he listens to me. Really listens to me, not just the typical nods and grunts. He even makes my lunch so that I won't eat from the food court."

"Girl, you're in so much trouble." Lori moved to the

opposite side of the rack Brinn had leaned against. "I was talking about his exterior. You're talking about his interior."

Brinn straightened and busied herself ordering the hangers by size, smallest to largest, from left to right. "I'm just noting that he has things going for him besides his hotness."

"You, my soon-to-be-former manager, are gonzo for this guy. And from the little bit I saw just now, I'd say that feeling is mutual."

"It's a temporary thing, nothing more. We're just enjoying each other's company until I leave town."

Lori's snort would have turned heads, if they'd had any to turn. "I bet he doesn't want you moving anywhere."

"That's a bet you'd lose. He helped me find a new apartment yesterday. He watched me write the check for my first month's rent, dated for two weeks from now. He told me he'd rent a pickup truck and help me move my stuff."

"For a manager with excellent people skills, you can be really dumb when it comes to your personal relationships. You're mistaking supportive behavior for happiness about a thing. Not the same at all."

"True, but—"

"Forget 'but,' let's bet instead."

Oh boy, this ought to be interesting. "Bet what?"

Lori tapped her index finger against her temple. "I've got it. I bet you a month's worth of Starbucks that before moving day rolls around, he asks you to stay."

A bet Lori was sure to lose.

Brinn extended her hand across the top of the floor rack. "You're on. I'll think of you when I'm in the middle of my million-dollar store, drinking my free daily latte."

"See, I already know your view of the future is a lie. There's no way you'd drink a latte on the sales floor."

She laughed at the well-intentioned dig at her store rules. Inside, the truth of Lori's words twisted around Brinn's heart. It didn't matter whether she pictured herself happily flying solo in a new city, or allowed herself to imagine a scenario where Davis continued to be part of her life. Neither would happen. Lori was right —Brinn's view of the future was a lie.

BRINN

The promise of a bright day—albeit a cold one— streamed through Brinn's bedroom window. Morning sunshine warmed her face, but nothing warmed the space beside her. She'd slept alone.

She patted around beneath the covers until she found her cell phone. Plenty of battery left. She hadn't accidentally muted the ringer either. A few quick taps revealed no missed texts or calls.

The last time she remembered seeing on the digital clock by her bed was 10:20. Shit. She should've stayed upright, on the couch, instead of getting horizontal. Fatigue had caught up with her and won.

Davis hadn't called or texted, but he might have come straight over after work, as he'd done several other times. What if she hadn't heard him knocking, then he'd left? Damn it. Stupid sleep had caused her to miss a night with him—and she didn't have enough nights left to squander any.

She'd rectify the situation right now, by ensuring it didn't happen again. A little advance planning to let him know she'd be awake and waiting for him after his shift tonight.

He answered her call with, "Hey, hang on a sec while I take care of something."

"Um, okay…" Her response was pointless. From the void-like air on the other end of the call, he'd obviously set his cell down and walked away. She pressed her phone tightly to her ear. Closed her eyes in hopes it'd heighten her hearing.

"Yeah, that works for me," he said to somebody other than her. "I'll swing by later. And I'll give you a call tonight."

Swing by where? Give who a call tonight? Try as she might, she couldn't hear a second voice. Just Davis's brief laugh at something the anonymous person must've said.

Then a corresponding *feminine* laugh.

Brinn's stomach lurched. The room felt as if it'd been sucked into a tornado. That's why he hadn't joined her in her bed last night—he'd had another woman in his. Now what? Hang up and give him the freedom he'd obviously been missing? She banged the heel of her hand against her forehead. Stupid, stupid, stupid...

"Still there?" His deep voice cut through her fog of self-loathing.

"Sorry for interrupting when you had company. You shouldn't have answered if you were in the middle of something."

"I wasn't. Barb was on her way out when my phone rang." He hadn't bothered to hide the fact that he was saying goodbye to not just a woman, but one with whom he'd previously admitted to having a long-standing fuck-buddy relationship. Asshole.

"Barb." God, that name tasted like poison. Brinn wanted to spit when she said it. "*Barb* was on her way out of your house at nine in the morning. I see."

Several seconds of thick silence passed before he answered. "I had a shitty fucking night last night. The owner rejected my menu proposal. Made it clear the changes I'd suggested were never going to happen. Then I spent the next nine hours making the same old fucking food. Food I'm going to be stuck making forever, unless I find somewhere else to work. Even if I do that, you know what's going to happen? More of the same, just under a different visionless boss. So when I left there, finally, I had to blow off some steam."

"And your choice for that was Barb."

"My choice was the 24-hour gym. Then a beer and hockey highlights. Then sleep. Alone." He exhaled low and long. "Jesus, Brinn."

She cringed. From across the city, she could practically see him rubbing the back of his neck. Trying to work out tension *she'd* just created, on top of his disappointment from yesterday.

"As for Barb being here so early, she stopped by to ask a favor. And before you dig yourself in deeper with the jealous-girlfriend bullshit, the favor was to make sure Alicia gets home from school, and to fix her some supper before I go to work. Barb usually works dayshift, but has to pull a weird split today. Alicia's your typical picky, moody teenager. Without a proper meal set in front of her, supper would probably be potato chips and hot chocolate."

She ought to spare him any more grief and end the call. But she couldn't—yet. "I'm really sorry your meeting didn't go the way you hoped. Your boss is a fool not to hand you the reins with the menu."

"Life goes on."

It did, and his would. More smoothly once she was out of it. "And I'm a different kind of sorry for acting like a bitchy jealous girlfriend."

"It happens."

"Well, it won't happen again with me." She closed her eyes and drew a fortifying breath. "To make sure of that, it's probably best if we don't get together again. My brain knows this is a casual, temporary thing, but my heart refuses to follow the memo. Whether you and Barb spent the night together or not shouldn't matter to me, but it does."

"We weren't together."

"I know." She sighed. "You're missing my point. You said I was acting like a jealous girlfriend, and you're right. Because that's how I feel—like I'm your girl-friend. I tried not to let it happen, but I got attached. I like you too much to keep seeing you."

"That's possibly the craziest thing a woman has ever said to me."

"I'd ask if there's a trophy for that, but it'd just be one more thing to pack."

He laughed—a brief one—then cleared his throat. "This is really what you want?"

"No. But it's the smart thing."

"You mean the safe thing."

"That too." She wiped her tears on the quilt. "I had a great time with you. Every day has been..." The rela-tionship of her dreams. "So much fun. Meeting you was the best Christmas present ever." With speedy fingers, she ended the call. With shaking hands, she turned off her phone.

Being smart and safe were currently the suckiest things on earth.

BRINN

Since Davis had entered her life, Brinn had opted for the closing shift more days than not. Her noon to nine thirty didn't match Davis's usual weekday schedule exactly, but it was close enough. Late-night sex, talking into the wee hours, waking up next to his strong, warm body, the lazy—or not so lazy—mornings together...she would miss those things. Starting tonight.

An announcement that mall hours had ended for the day echoed in the too-quiet corridor. Thank goodness. There'd been no TGIF in this Friday shift—it'd dragged at a snail's pace. Low sales and budgets at this time of year didn't allow for additional staff, so she'd spent the last three hours alone in the store. Alone in her head. Neither were fun places to be at the moment.

Head down, she dragged the rolling racks in from the lease line. A hissed curse escaped when her hip connected with the corner of a shelf. She jerked at the streak of pain shooting down her leg, clipping a floor mannequin in the process.

"Shit!" she said, this time at full volume, as the life-size dummy careened sideways. She let go of the rolling rack and lunged for the mannequin clearly bent on escape.

"Got it." The unmistakable deep voice came from behind the mannequin. Another second and it would've crashed spectacularly against the neighboring store's bay display window. Davis to the rescue, once again.

"Thanks."

"No problem," he said, moving in tandem with her.

She busied herself with the racks and the roll-down door. Anything to avoid meeting his warm hazel eyes. To spare her heart the pain that would come from seeing his handsome face.

"Stop." He reached out to halt the door's descent when she pulled the metal rungs downward.

"I need to close the store. Mall security gets a little lax at this time of year and I don't want to be the last person making the long, dark walk to the edge of the parking lot. Especially on a Friday night."

"I'll walk you to your car."

Still averting her gaze, she tugged at the door—which didn't budge.

"Brinn, look at me."

She shook her head. "You're supposed to be at work."

"I called in."

"Because of last night?"

"No. Because of you."

She raised her head and got instantly caught in his determined gaze. "Other than a fit of klutziness, I'm fine."

"Never said I thought otherwise. I'm not here to

check on you, I'm here to give you something." He released the overhead door to retrieve a box from inside his coat. "For you," he said, offering it up.

Bigger than every girl's dream of a ring box. Less than half the size of a shoe box. The red package tempted her, but she kept her fingers safely curled around the metal rungs of the door. "Why?"

"Because I wanted to." The same reason he'd given when she asked why he'd bought her a Christmas present. He stepped inside the store, removed her hand from the door and pulled it down, closing them in together. "If you want me to leave, I will. After you open number one."

"Number one?" Damn his mystique and pretty presents. How was she supposed to resist? She accepted the box, shivering when his fingers trailed over her palm.

"Number one of ten."

"There are *ten* things in this box?"

His smile further melted her resolve. "Open it and see."

Sighing, she traced the perimeter of the shiny red box. "This is very fancy."

"Presentation, babe."

Of course. Even when he served up scrambled eggs or a simple sandwich, he did it with style. Ketchup in a little bowl on the side, rather than simply putting the bottle on the table. Pickles pared to resemble palm trees the day she'd wished out loud for them to be on a tropical island instead of watching snow pile up mercilessly.

She wiggled the top upward until it popped free of its rigid base. "Fortune cookies?"

"Yeah. One for each day you're still here." He poked at the novelties, turning them over in place. "There's number one. Open it."

"Okay…" She picked up the cookie marked with a red *1* and broke it open. Crumbs floated down, into the box. She grasped the end of the enclosed strip and pulled gently.

Spend the next ten days with me.

"How did you do this?"

"Right-handed. Wanted you to be able to read it."

"Smartass," she said, nudging him with her arm.

He caught her elbow, relieved her of the box and broken cookie, then pulled her closer. Her other arm stuck up from between their chests, the handwritten message pinched tightly between her thumb and index finger.

"I made the cookies. And the fortunes."

That covered the *how*. "Why?"

"I thought you'd like them. At your parents' on Christmas Day, you got so much enjoyment out of the party crackers. The way you jumped when they snapped, even though you knew it would happen. How excited you were to read the fortunes inside, your genuine attempts to make them relevant to real life.

Babe, I could've watched you pop those crackers open all day."

To hear him say things like that...gah. Did he have any idea how sweet he was?

"And the night at your apartment when you insisted we order Chinese instead of going out to buy groceries for your barren refrigerator. You couldn't wait to bust into those fortune cookies. You blushed so hard when you read yours, but you didn't want to tell me what it said."

"It was embarrassing." *You will marry your lover*, it had read.

"Only because you believe there's truth in the things."

"And you knew that," she whispered. "That's why I didn't want you to see it."

"Do you still believe the fortunes come true?"

The correct answer here was *no*. "I think fate might have a hand in them. It's not impossible."

"So fucking sweet." His sexy grin ruined her for all other potential smiling suitors. "Then give fate the credit for the one you're holding, Brinn. You're here for ten more days. Spend them with me. No more stupid misunderstandings or premature goodbyes. What do you say?"

If she said yes, he'd break her heart. Wide open, with jagged pieces spinning out in all directions. Not intentionally or maliciously, but he'd do it, nonetheless.

There'd be so many chinks when she tried piecing it back together, it would never be the same. Stay firm with the goodbye she'd said earlier, that's what she needed to do.

"Yes. I say yes."

DAVIS

"Can I open today's cookie now?" Brinn smiled at him with glistening, deep-pink lips. "Pretty please?"

"I see how it is. Take advantage of me first thing in the morning, then hit me up for whatever you want, knowing I'll be powerless to resist you."

"Powerless to resist me? In that case, I'm rethinking my request. I'm sure I can ask for something bigger than a fortune cookie."

"Ask away, babe." He wrapped his arms around her after she crawled up and snuggled in at his side. "If it's within my means, the answer is yes."

"Wow. That must have been the best blowjob ever."

"Going with a yes on that." He'd woken to the sensation of Brinn's weight on his chest, then her tight pussy sinking onto his morning wood.

Either she'd just had one hell of an erotic dream, or she'd played with herself before she climbed on top, because it took her all of about sixty seconds to come—

and come hard. Then she'd slid down his body and finished him off with her mouth. Between sucks and licks, she'd told him she could taste herself on his cock, and how much it turned her on. So fucking hot.

Luckily, they'd both had recent checkups, and no sexual partners since. He always wore condoms. Always. Even when a woman said she was on the Pill. Until Brinn. He'd been totally on board when she suggested foregoing the latex for the duration of their time together. Yet another of his personal rules broken where she was concerned. And he didn't regret a single one.

"Did you think of something bigger than the fortune cookie?" he asked, pressing his lips to the top of her head. He'd learned to control the visibility of his emotions a long time ago. Right now, it took every ounce of that control to keep his heart rate at a normal pace. He'd basically given her carte blanche.

She propped up on her elbow and looked down at his face. "Aren't you afraid of what I might ask for?"

"Not in the slightest."

"All right. I want…" She worried her bottom lip between her teeth before letting it slide free, along with the rest of her request. "To know more about you."

"What do you want to know?" If he thought about her practically every waking minute? If he loved her?

"It's a big question. You might not want to answer."

"Only one way to find out." This is what he wanted

—for Brinn to put the pressure on, give him an excuse to admit the depth of his feelings.

"Okay…" She traced his collarbone with a light touch, focusing on her fingers and his skin beneath them as she spoke. "Are you where you want to be? In life, I mean."

"Not the question I was expecting."

Her gaze lifted. She remained silent, but emotion filled her eyes. Ah. She *had* asked the question he'd expected—just indirectly.

So he'd answer it. "I like where my life's at right now." He caught the wavy section of dirty-blonde hair that'd fallen over her shoulder and tucked it behind her ear. "If things stayed the way they are today, this very minute, I'd be pretty damn content."

"I don't think spending the rest of your life naked in bed is a realistic option."

"Naked and in bed *with you,*" he said, cupping the back of her neck and gently tugging her on top of him.

"Even less realistic. Unless we win the lottery in that fantasy world of yours."

"How about getting an inheritance? My grandfather's in his eighties. I could get that call any day."

She pushed up from his chest, staring at with wide-open eyes. "Seriously? That could happen?"

"Yeah. I don't know exactly how much it'll be, but he built one of the most successful law firms in the country from scratch, so I'm sure it'll be a lot. Enough for us to stay naked in bed for several years, at least."

She nudged him—and not in an affectionate or amused way—then shifted back to her position along his side. "I wasn't asking about the money, Davis. I was referring to your grandfather being on death's door. Was he sick the last time you saw him?"

He should've known she'd home in on the family connection, not the impending windfall. "No, he wasn't sick. Gramps was in better health than most men half his age. I'm sure I would've heard if that had changed."

"How long has it been since you saw your family?"

"Six thorn-in-my-side-free years."

"You don't really feel that way," she said in a voice as soft as her silky skin.

"You can't understand it because you could never feel that way about your family. Like I told you before, my family's nothing like yours."

"I'm not arguing that point. And I know the unhappiness you experienced for so many years is very real. But I don't believe you've hardened your heart where your family is concerned. Not entirely, anyway."

Oh man, the way she was looking at him, as if she were seeing right through him. Yeah, he'd kind of wanted an excuse to spill his guts. About his feelings for *her*, not about this. Yet he was the one who'd mentioned his family in the first place. Now he was trapped between a beautiful blonde and a box of old ghosts. Shit.

She leaned in and kissed him. Not a sexy kiss, but an intimate one. Tender. Deep. The kind that lingered, even after she'd pulled away. Her perfect touch graced his head, further diffusing his fight-or-flight impulse. "If you didn't care at all, you would've stuck with 'my grandfather' or maybe even something less personal. But you referred to him as Gramps."

"Old habit."

"Ever think about calling him? Maybe start a new habit?"

Yeah, he thought about it from time to time. Self-preservation always kicked in before he made the mistake of completing the call. "I know you think it's a good idea. One that'll have a movie-of-the-week ending where I reunite with my family and everybody lives in harmony. That's not going to happen, Brinn. Don't look for a happily ever after where there'll never be one."

"Okay," she whispered, withdrawing her hands from his skin.

"Fuck, I didn't mean to raise my voice. Not to you. Not ever to you." He scooped her closer, then rolled their bodies so he was on top, pinning her beneath him. "I wish every real-life story got a happy ending. Especially mine, now that you're in it."

"Some wishes come true, you know."

He had to laugh, even though it spoiled the moment. He kissed the crease that'd formed between her eyebrows and freed her from the cage of his body. "Go get today's fortune cookie."

Still giving him the side-eye at his ill-timed burst of laughter, she shuffled to the edge of the bed. Sexy ass swaying, she crossed the room to his dresser, where she'd left the remaining fortune cookies in a tidy row.

He patted the empty space where her body should be. "Bring it over here and open it."

His good girl obeyed, sliding into place beside him and cracking the cookie in two.

"I'll take care of this mess," he said, using his tongue to clean the crumbs that'd fluttered down to her breasts. As much as he wanted to linger, he resisted. He needed to see her face when she read the fortune he'd written seven days ago.

"*Some wishes come true.* Oh my god, Davis...I can't believe this."

"Pretty coincidental."

"See, I'm turning you into a believer." She smiled, and it could've lit up the city, it was so damn beautiful and bright. "Coincidence is just a hop, skip and jump from fate."

Chapter Ten

DAVIS

Davis checked the dish in the oven. Baked ziti with chorizo and spinach—looking as good as it smelled. Salad and fresh bread were ready to go. The layered panna cotta he'd made for dessert was waiting in the fridge. The kitchen was clean and the wine was breathing. Everything would be ready when Brinn got home from her last day of work.

When Brinn got home. The thought came so automatically. Not surprisingly, though. He'd spent almost every night with her over the past month, sometimes at her apartment, but mostly here, in his home. She fit here. In his house, in his life. But tonight might be the last of their time together. He'd know soon enough.

He set two places on the corner of the breakfast bar. More intimate than sitting across from each another.

This way, their knees touched, their arms brushed, and he had a close-up view of her enjoyment of the meal.

Seeing people appreciate his food had always given him a kick. With Brinn, it'd become an addiction. He craved her reactions. The way her big eyes would widen when she tasted whatever it was he'd prepared. The sight of her sexy lips moving as she chewed. And the sounds she made—fuck. Sometimes he thought she might be on the verge of coming.

Cooking for her had reignited his passion in the kitchen. The fact that he routinely had *her* as his personal appetizer and dessert in this room didn't hurt either. If she left tomorrow, as planned, his kitchen would never be the same.

He placed the tenth and final fortune cookie on her plate. She'd loved his messages so far. Her face lit up each time she'd read one. Sometimes she'd giggled. Sometimes she'd gotten quiet and the tip of her nose had gone pink.

The tenth fortune required an answer. They'd grown to know each other pretty well, yet he honestly didn't know what she'd say when she read tonight's message.

A *tap tap* on the front door preceded a gust of cold air that accompanied her inside. No point in chastising her for the soft knock. At least she'd walked in, instead of waiting outside. Even that had taken some convincing on his part.

"Hey, babe." In a couple strides he was behind her, helping her out of her jacket. "How was today?"

"Good. Slow for business, but busy with getting everything in order for whoever they bring in to manage that store. My assistant is good, but she's not ready to run the show."

"Nobody's going to be as good as you." He hugged her from behind, nuzzling her soft hair before tucking it aside for access to her neck. Subtle fragrance filled his nose, and head. "You're wearing the perfume I bought you. I thought that was against your rules at work."

"It is." She turned and wrapped her arms around his neck. "I was a bad girl and broke the rules." She pressed her sweet curves against his body and whispered in his ear, "Good thing I didn't get caught."

Blood diverted from the brain in his head to the one in his pants. "Incorrect. You did get caught—by me."

"And are you going to write me up, or let me off with an oral reprimand?"

"Oh, there's going to be oral. But it's going to *get* you off, not let you off."

She gasped as he swept her off the floor, into his arms. She snuggled against his chest for the short trip to the bedroom, another soft gasp escaping when he set her on top of his bed. "It's so beautiful in here..."

"It is now," he said, crouching before her as she took in the dozens of burning candles and vases with single red roses he'd placed around the room. He reached for the remote on the nightstand and hit the *play* button.

Her lips parted when the music started. "I thought you didn't like country music."

"But you do." The candlelight cast a soft glow over the room, and wrapped around Brinn like a golden aura. "And tonight is all about you." From his position between her legs, he unzipped one of her boots, then the other, and set them aside. He cupped her face in his palms and kissed her. The soft kind. Slow and long. Fucking delicious.

Between them, she found his button and zipper. Snuck her hand inside his boxers and wrapped her talented little fingers around his dick.

"Stand up," she whispered between kisses. "I want your cock in my mouth."

"Whatever my good girl wants—" He rose, pushed his pants to his hips and rubbed the engorged tip over her bottom lip, then inside her warm, willing mouth. "She gets."

Palms braced against his abdomen, she looked up at him with wide, eager eyes. She leaned in, changed angles.

"You want more?" he asked, and she nodded. He gave her another inch. Then another. "You want it all?"

Another nod. Wrists and palms pressed together, she raised her hands, nudged one of his.

Goddamn, she wanted this now, tonight? He circled both her wrists with one hand and drew her arms above her head. "You want it like this, babe?" He pushed deeper, until every last fraction of an inch filled her mouth. "You want me fucking your face, taking control of your pretty mouth?"

Her hummed consent vibrated along his shaft. Every drop of available blood rushed to his rock-fucking-hard dick. He withdrew as slowly as he'd entered, pulling out completely, then filled her mouth in one smooth motion.

"Fuck, your mouth feels so good." He retreated, pushed inside again, groaning at the tight seal of her lips around his dick, the erotic slide of her tongue. No way could he go slow and gentle. Not with Brinn looking up at him while he fucked her face.

Jesus, the picture she made. Pink cheeks, glassy eyes, hands shackled above her head. Submitting to whatever he chose to give her. Eagerly taking his cock as he thrust between her full, glossy lips, over and over.

"I could come right now, and fuck, babe, it's tempting. I'd love to bury my cock in your face and come down your throat. Watch you swallow every fucking drop before I let you go. But not yet. Too many things I need to do to you first."

She whimpered when he released her hands and left her mouth empty. "I would've liked that."

"Yeah, well, you're going to love what I do to you next." He caught her hands, one in each of his, and pulled her to her feet, against his body. "I'm going to touch every inch of you." Swaying to the slow music, he peeled her top up and over her head. "Kiss you all over." He unhooked her bra and slid the straps down her arms. "Starting here..." He lowered his head, sucked one hard nipple into his mouth while he strummed the other with his thumb.

Her fingers splayed across the back of his head and she pulled him tighter to her breast. "You're right, I love that."

"Me too, babe. I love your tits. Your perfect pink nipples, all hard and begging to be bitten."

"If they're begging, you should give them what they want."

They'd barely gotten started and she was killing him. He switched sides, flicking the hard peak with the tip of his tongue before closing his mouth over it, and grazing it with his teeth.

"That's a nibble, not a bite."

He growled at the taunt. Caught the little bullet between his teeth and gave it hard pressure. Really fucking hard. Her throaty moan filled his ears, and his hips jerked forward involuntarily. Soon. He had to be inside her soon.

He headed south, hands and mouth moving over her stomach and abdomen as he pushed her jeans and panties down and off. "What about here?" He wiggled his tongue against her clit. "And here." He slid a finger into her pussy, groaning at the tight heat. "Hard or soft, babe? Tell me how you want it."

"Any way. Every way." Her hips rolled forward to meet his mouth and fingers. "Just don't stop."

"That's my plan." He hooked his arm behind her knees and scooped her up, then laid her on the bed. "I need you this way." He nudged her legs apart, trailed his fingers all over her soft skin. "Wide open. All mine."

"I am." Barely a whisper, her voice. As if she didn't want him to hear it.

He stripped off his clothes and settled between her creamy thighs. Her warm, sweet scent surrounded him. But he could get closer. He wrapped his arms around her hips and pulled her pussy tight against his face. No teasing this time. He needed to devour her.

He always told her he loved the taste of her, and it was the truth. Sweet when he licked and suckled. A spicy tang when she came. He needed that tonight. Needed her completely undone for him.

He slid his hand up her body. Palmed one perfect tit, rolled her nipple between his fingers. A firm pinch, the kind that made her arch and squirm and moan. Oh yeah.

"More," she said, tilting her hips.

His cock was already hard as a fucking battering ram, but her breathless tone made it harder. She drove him crazy when she sounded that way—sex-drunk and desperate. Because of him.

Warm, tight heat welcomed him as he filled her with two fingers. She opened wider for him, a silent plea for even more. Her whole body arched when he added a third finger. Her thighs shook and pussy rocked against his face as he stroked and sucked. She was close. Very close.

"Touch my ass."

He twisted his wrist, slid his pinkie finger lower and pressed it against her tight little ring.

"Inside," she whispered.

Oh fuck yeah. He was all over that. He wiggled his finger, massaging until he breached her rim. Slow and steady, he pushed inside while bearing down on her clit with his tongue.

"God, Davis, god..." Her hands gripped the top of his head while she shook and bucked and softly moaned.

He'd lose it if he looked up at her, but he fucking had to risk it. Brinn coming was the most erotic thing in the world. Her curves as she writhed. Rock-hard nipples still begging for attention. A deep flush coloring her chest and cheeks. The closed, fluttering eyelids and parted lips.

Sometimes he kept going after she finished, just to hear her shrieks and giggles. Not this time. He brought her down gently, then kissed his way up to her mouth, covering her with his body.

"So fucking beautiful," he said, groaning as he slid home. Buried deep in her pussy, he stilled, savoring the way her body hugged him tight, yet fit him perfectly. "You feel like you were made for me."

She wrapped her legs around his hips, cupped the back of his head and pulled him down. "Maybe I was," she whispered against his lips.

Yeah, maybe. They'd figure it out. Right now he wanted to show her how he felt, not talk. He rocked his hips, moving inside her and eliciting a soft moan. Mint and Brinn, a delicious combo he couldn't get enough of, mixed with his breath. An invitation he'd never refuse.

He sealed their lips together while stroking in and out of her body. The tip of her tongue teased his, and he met it with sweeping strokes. Skin to skin, connected everywhere—fucking amazing.

Brinn arched to take him deeper. Sparks flared beneath her nails as they dug into his ass. Body shuddering beneath him, she breathed his name into his mouth. Coming for him. Around him. So hot. So completely fucking hot.

Fire roared to life in his balls. A couple more strokes, max, before he joined her.

"Turn me over," she whispered. "I want you to fuck my ass."

Jesus, just hearing the words almost did him in. He pulled back enough to look in her eyes, get a read on her face. "You sure?"

"More than sure. Turn me over."

Pulling out of her sweet pussy was torture, until he looked down at her gorgeous naked body. Waves of dirty-blonde hair fanned over his bed. Full lips swollen from sucking and kissing smiled up at him. A glow tinted her fair skin. Her deep-pink nipples stood hard and her shapely curves begged for his touch.

He kissed his way from her lips to her hips, then gently rolled her onto her stomach. Goddamn, what a beautiful sight. He crouched over her and brushed her hair to one side. "I'm crazy about you, Brinn." He kissed the sensitive spot below her ear while stroking between her legs. "I'll do anything and everything to make you feel good. And stop immediately if it doesn't." He dragged her body's natural lube from her pussy to her ass, used it to ease his middle finger inside. "Relax and trust me, baby. I promise to take care of you."

Eyes closed, she bit into her bottom lip and nodded as he added a second finger.

He rocked in and out, gently working into a rhythm that matched her responses. "Tell me how it feels."

"Kind of hot...but good."

"Yeah, that's how it always feels for me when I finger your ass, except take out the 'kind of hot' and replace it with 'insanely fucking hot,'" he said, and she giggled. A very good sign. "I'm going to grab the lube."

"Okay," she said as he slipped from her body and the bed. "Notice how I didn't ask about it?"

The question stalled him for a second before it clicked. Their first night together, he'd told her that when the time and guy were right, she wouldn't even think about the lube.

He grabbed the tube from the drawer, then leaned down to steal another taste of her mouth. "Did you hear the part where I'm crazy about you?"

"I did. I'm crazy about you too."

Good. All good. He warmed a generous amount of lube between his palms while resuming his position over the backs of her thighs. He slid his hands along the valley of her ass. Massaged her sexy curves until he'd coated every inch with the slick stuff. His dick was so goddamn hard and erect, it could probably hold up the roof.

He needed inside her. Now. "I'm going to go nice and slow."

Beautiful profile pressed to the bed, she nodded. "I want this. With you."

He bit back a groan when his cock made its first pass through the slippery valley between her cheeks. Back and forth, he slid, coating his cock with the lube and getting closer to her ass with each stroke. Even this put him on edge. He was so tightly wound, he'd be lucky to get an inch of his dick inside her before he came.

She tilted her hips, grabbed her ass and—holy fuck, give him strength—spread herself open, revealing her tight little ring.

Didn't matter how many times he'd seen it. Up close and very personal, with his fingers and tongue. Brinn loved ass play, and he fucking loved playing with her ass. But this time... Jesus, this time.

He guided his cock into place. Gave a hint of pressure, enough to watch the tip disappear. He splayed his palm across her lower back. Then he rocked. In a fraction. Out. In a bit more. As gently as humanly possible, given the extreme fucking sexiness of the woman beneath him.

She moaned—a low, throaty sound that sent a spike of fire straight to his balls—when the head of his cock fully breached her rim. "Is that all of it?"

"No, babe. A lot more where that came from." He pushed deeper, one slow inch at a time. "Got half my cock in your sexy ass now. Still want more?"

"Yes, more, I want it all." Her soft voice and moans were killing him. Destroying his thinly held control.

He cupped her hips and thrust deeper. Deeper. Until the last of his cock disappeared and his balls hung against her pussy. "So tight. Brinn, baby, you feel so goddamn good. Soon as I move, it's going to be game over."

"I don't care how long it lasts, just fuck me."

He curled his fingertips into her flesh and eased back. Not all the way. Just enough to feel the hot squeeze of her ass taking his dick when he thrust back in, balls-deep. "Jesus..."

"Don't stop—" Bad little good girl that she was, she rolled her hips and pushed backward, taking him even deeper. "Do it again."

Oh yeah, he could do that. He was happy to do that. And do it again. And again. Heat raced through his body, lighting every nerve ending on fire. The inferno spread to his balls, then to his cock, buried deep in her hot ass.

"Fuuuck..." he groaned, rutting on her like an animal in heat before folding himself over her back. He pressed his lips against her neck. Breathed her in while nuzzling her soft skin. "You okay?"

"Much better than okay. Is it always like that?" she asked, hugging his arm tighter around her waist as he withdrew from her ass.

"Like what? Me neglecting to make you come?"

"Geez. Am I that demanding that you think the other two times don't count?"

He had to chuckle at her affronted tone. "Oh, they counted. They were fucking hot. But why settle for two when you can have three, right?"

"Good point," she said, wiggling onto her side so they were nose-to-nose. "Maybe we should start over again."

Now he full-out laughed. "Feed a guy dinner first, wouldya, my beautiful nymphomaniac?"

"Hmm..." She tapped one manicured fingertip against her smiling lips. "I suppose I can wait that long. But only if you promise me dessert."

"Hold that thought," he said, practically jumping up from the bed. "I'll be back in a sec."

No point in waiting. Timing was as important as presentation, and there was no better time for his question than after wicked, connected sex. He trotted down the hall to the kitchen, snagged the fortune cookie and was back in the bedroom in under a minute.

"What was that all about?"

He dropped onto the bed alongside her. Propped on

one arm, he offered up the cookie on his other hand. "Dessert."

"Oh." Her voice was as soft as the fingers brushing his palm when she picked it up. "This is the last one..." She worried her bottom lip between her teeth while blinking faster than normal. "I was going to save it until after I move."

Shit. That wouldn't work. He cupped her chin, tilted her face upward so he could look in her eyes. "I need you to crack it open tonight."

She nodded, then pushed up to a position mirroring his. In the small gap between their bodies, she broke the cookie in two. Almond-colored crumbs dotted the navy duvet. In what seemed like super-slow motion, she pulled the strip of paper free of its crisp casing. Stared at the fortune. Then stared over at him. But said nothing.

What the hell—had he had a moment of insanity? Had he scribbled something completely whacko on the note, instead of the message he'd intended?

"I don't know what to say, Davis." Her gaze dropped to the small note. "'*Stay.*' What does that mean?"

"It's a verb, the opposite of go or leave. An action word with no action."

She didn't smile or giggle at his intended joke. Just quietly asked, "But what does it *mean*?"

"I met you at my least favorite time of the year. Christmas, the season devoted to celebrating family relationships, which I no longer have because I walked away from a line of cold, competitive assholes more interested in one-upping each other than having a warm feeling about anything. Add to that, the fact that my house had been robbed, and I was in a foul mood to end all foul moods. Until I spotted you."

Her eyelids fluttered, then she met his eyes again. "That was a great night."

"One of the best." He leaned in and brushed a kiss over her lips. "I invited you to my house, planning on a few fun hours together. Didn't take me long to realize one night with you wouldn't be enough. By the time we got back from your parents' house Christmas Day, I knew I wanted to keep seeing you until you left town. I thought it'd be safe, getting involved with you that way, without any pressure to commit to 'more' down the road."

"I really hate your family for souring you against meaningful relationships."

"Yeah, well, you un-soured me." The edge of the paper rasped his palm as he covered her fidgety hand with his. "I want you to stay here and see what happens between us."

"Here, meaning...?"

"In St. Catherines."

"I'm moving tomorrow. I start at my new position on Tuesday."

"But you don't have to. Your current store doesn't have a replacement yet, and your apartment hasn't been rented."

"I—" Long, soft curls tumbled forward, over her shoulder as she shook her head. "This is big, and I need a few minutes to collect my thoughts," she said, shimmying out of reach, then off the bed. "Meet you in the kitchen?"

"Yeah, of course." He collected his clothes from the floor and leaned in to steal another kiss before giving her the space she'd requested.

She was right, this was big. A step he hadn't planned to take—ever—but one that felt natural with Brinn. He'd kind of sweated writing that message ten days ago. Because, what if? What if things went south between them before the tenth day arrived? It'd been a risk. But each day, the lingering doubts faded a bit more.

Admittedly, leaving this question until the eleventh hour wasn't the wisest plan. And asking her to pass up a promotion, even temporarily, was a lot.

With her skills, another opportunity wouldn't be far off. Hell, she might even end up at the other mall here in St. Catherines, running her company's newly renovated flagship store. She'd already mentioned the possibility of returning someday, as retail managers often bounced from store to store. Hopefully she'd rather stay and wait it out than leave and bounce her way back.

In the kitchen, he pulled on his boxers and jeans. Got to work assembling their dinner on plates. Pouring the wine. Lighting the candles. How many times had his parents used words like *romantic* and *dreamer* about him? More than he could count. They'd been right, even if they'd tainted the characteristics with negativity and sarcasm.

"Wow, it smells amazing in here."

He looked up from grating fresh Provolone over their meals. After everything they'd just done in his bedroom, his cock ought to be down and done for a while. Not the case. One look at Brinn in black leggings and a formfitting, pale-blue top that showed off her curves and his dick was wide awake.

"Come, sit." He pulled out a chair and nodded at her plate. "I think you're going to like this."

"That's a given. Everything you make is mouthgasm inducing."

"Hell of an endorsement." He took the remaining seat. "But I can't take all the credit for the food. I have this new muse who inspires me."

She smiled from behind the glass of wine she'd just sipped. "What does she do to inspire you?"

"Gives incredible head, tastes like heaven when she comes on my tongue, has the sexiest tits in the world," he said, winking.

"Ah. So your muse is a porn star."

"She could be." He slid his hand from her knee to the top of her thigh while leaning in to kiss her neck. "But she's currently all mine."

Brinn's expressive face held no secrets. At least not from him. She had several smiles, from sultry to sweet, with all kinds of emotions in between. Right now, none of them graced her pretty face.

"Hey." He caught her hands in his. "It's more than sex."

"I know."

"Good." Something had chased her happiness away, though, and if it was him, he damn sure wanted to know how. "Talk to me."

"You said 'currently.' I'm *currently* all yours."

"It's just a word."

"It's not the word I need to hear. Neither was 'St. Catherines' when I asked you what you meant by 'stay here.'"

"I'm an intelligent guy, Brinn, but I'd rather hear exactly what's on your mind than try to read between the lines."

"Ever since college, I've been waiting for Mr. Right to come along. I know it's old-fashioned, but I want somebody to go home to every night. Somebody I can count on. A man who makes me happy, and appreciates that I make him happy too."

"Nothing wrong with that."

"No, there's not. What's wrong is that I've made it my number-one priority. After college, I should've gone out and found a good position in my field. Instead, I took a going-nowhere minimum-wage job in a retail store, just so I could continue to be with my then-boyfriend. He wasn't Mr. Right, obviously, but I managed to work my way up to the manager position at the store, so I had that achievement, at least."

"Same company you're with now?" he asked when she paused.

"Yes."

He nodded and waited for her to continue. "Congratulations" probably wasn't the response she wanted to hear at the moment, even if he was impressed that she'd made something out of next-to-nothing.

"I did well, and my DM moved me to a higher-volume store in a different mall. That's where I met Liam. He was managing a sporting goods chain store near the food court."

"More proof that eating at the food court is bad news."

At that, she laughed. Even smiled briefly. "Then he got bumped to the mall here. A demotion. A couple months later, I requested a transfer so I could follow him, even though it meant managing a significantly lower-volume store. All because Liam dangled the 'I love you, move here so we can see more of each other and *maybe* live happily ever after' bait."

He schooled his face, but inside, he grimaced. His proposal rang pretty damn close to Liam's. And Davis knew how that attempt at a happily ever after had faired. The asshole had fucking cheated on her. No surprise Brinn was hesitant after being burned.

"I'm not Liam," he said, brushing the pad of his thumb over her lip. "I'd never hurt you the way he did."

"I know. But—" Her breath hitched as she bit back whatever would have followed. "I was willing to move down the ladder to be with a guy, then further down if necessary, to avoid seeing him anymore. I was just lucky enough to get promoted instead."

"Not lucky. You earned it. Because you're great at your job."

"Yes, I am. And it's time I focused on my individual success as much as my desire for a relationship. I need to base my decisions on more than wishful thinking." A frown played across her trembling lips. "That's why I'm moving tomorrow."

Shit. This was not going the way he'd hoped. He released one hand to wipe the tear that'd rolled down her cheek. "Leaving can't be the best choice if it's making you unhappy."

"If I stayed, it would be because of you. Me, hoping this thing between us turns out to be the big love of my lifetime. That's not a fair expectation of any man, especially one who doesn't want the same thing. You asking me to forfeit an important career opportunity to extend our status quo for an undetermined amount of time isn't a fair expectation either."

"You're right. But it's all I can offer right now."

She threw her arms around his neck and buried her face against his neck. "I don't want this to be our last night together."

"Neither do I."

"Then let's find an alternative. It's only a two-hour drive, we can keep seeing each other."

He eased free of her vise-like hug. Cupped her beautiful face between his palms. "When are we going to see each other, Brinn? I work late most nights. Rarely have weekends off. You frequently put in extra hours, and that's probably going to increase with the busier store and additional responsibilities. We'd be lucky to coordinate one day a week together. You said it yourself—you want somebody to go home to every night."

"I wish that somebody could be you," she whispered, pressing her forehead against his.

No point in telling her he wished the same thing. Instead, he showed her, with his mouth on hers. With his hands in her hair. For one more night.

Chapter Eleven

DAVIS

ANOTHER DAY IN THE BAG. THAT WAS IT, THE extent of his feelings about his Friday night shift. He used to leave work feeling pumped and positive, or pissed because the wheels had flown off in all directions. High, low, or somewhere in the middle, he'd always felt *something* about his job. Until lately. Now it all just fell flat.

Davis scrolled through the preset stations on the radio while making the autopilot drive from the restaurant to his house. Top-forty, rock, club mixes—none of the music grabbed him.

Work rut. Music rut. Must be the time of year. Long, dark days and the deep freeze of February made it hard to be enthusiastic. Time to add something new to the daily grind.

He pressed the search button on the radio and waited for it to find the next signal. He'd start with random musical input. Tomorrow he'd haul his lazy ass out of the house. Shake things up, get out of his rut. Force himself to rejoin the land of the living.

The radio picked up a station and music filled the car. Country—pass. The twang all sounded the same to him. He reached for the button, stopping short when recognition sparked.

Country music had never appealed to him, but he knew this song. Knew it well. Brinn loved it. He'd copied it from her playlist and they'd swayed to it in his bedroom. He'd undressed her while it played, then laid her on his bed and made her come with his fingers and mouth. Fucking beautiful, his Brinn. Sweet yet so damn sexy. He wasn't about to forget this song. Or her.

They'd said their goodbyes three weeks ago. They'd texted since she moved, but each time, the exchange got shorter. Less personal and more awkward. His last attempt at communication had been one way, when he messaged her but didn't receive a reply. On Valentine's Day. The silence told him plenty. So did the fact that he'd counted the days without contact.

Shit. Yeah, they'd clicked. A lot. Inside the bedroom and out of it. But it was a month of his life. He should've moved on already. He should at least *want* to move on.

The dashboard clock read 11:20 as he pulled into his driveway. Late, but not crazy late. Several inches of powdery snow had accumulated since he left for work mid-afternoon. Normally, he'd take ten minutes to shovel the sidewalk in front of his house and the neighbors'. Right now he didn't give a shit about anything other than getting inside and on the phone.

He locked the front door and shrugged out of his coat. His on-the-fly toss missed the mark, sending his coat and keys sliding off the arm of the leather couch to hit the floor with a light thud. He liked things orderly, but right now he couldn't care less about the pile on the living room floor. Or anything other than connecting with Brinn.

In his bedroom, he propped the pillows against the headboard and settled in on top of the duvet. To text or call. A text would be easier. Pose the question, wait for her answer, go from there.

Easy was good. Familiar. Keeping it simple had been his MO with women for years. But nothing about his next move was familiar or usual. He'd never pursued a woman after walking away. He'd never had this hole in his life after he let one go.

Fuck it. Since he was going down a new road, he might as well use a new approach. He brought up her contact info and tapped the "call" icon. Generic ringing on his end, but two hours away, on her end, birds were chirping. And that made him smile for the first time all day.

"Because it's a joyful sound, and I hope all the calls I get are

happy ones," had been the reason she cited when he asked why she'd chosen the sound for her ringtone.

He'd never met anybody as genuinely optimistic as Brinn. The quality made her naïve at times. A bit unrealistic in her expectations, maybe. But it was also part of her spirit. Her vitality. Characteristics to which he'd quickly become addicted during their time together.

On his end, the phone rang a third time. Shit, maybe he'd called too late.

"Davis...hi." Brinn's sweet voice filled his ear halfway through the fourth ring. "This is a surprise."

That was on him. Standing in the door of her new apartment, she'd wrapped her arms around his neck and buried her face against his neck. Instead of saying goodbye, she'd suggested for a second time that they keep things going, try a long-distance relationship. He'd shut her down. Not in a dick way, but a very final rejection nonetheless.

"I was driving home from work just now, flipping through the stations on the radio, trying to find something good to listen to. That country song you like came on. The one that was playing when I undressed you. The night before you moved."

"Burnin' Bed," she whispered.

"Yeah, that's the one."

"I'll always remember that night."

"So will I," he said. Two hundred kilometers separated them, yet the air charged as if she were beside him on the bed, staring into his soul with those big blue eyes of hers. "I want to see you, Brinn. I have tomorrow night off. How about I come up and make you dinner?"

"I can't."

"Because of work? I thought the mall closed at six on Saturdays."

"It does...but I have plans afterward. The manager next door and I arranged to grab dinner and a drink in the mall restaurant. Commiserating about post-holiday returns and unrealistic corporate sales budgets, exciting stuff like that. I wouldn't feel right canceling last minute."

"Of course, I get it. How about after that? We can catch a movie, hang out and relax, whatever you want to do." Silence stretched between them. If not for the faint sound of her breathing, he might've thought the call had dropped.

"I'm sorry, I can't do that either."

The blood that'd diverted to his cock minutes earlier chilled instantly. "It's not dinner, a drink and shop talk, is it? You've got a date."

"Maybe."

"There's no *maybe*. It's a date or it's not. If you're trying to spare my feelings—don't."

"I believe that in your world, Davis, there's no *maybe* about dating. When *you* ask a woman out, it's a given there'll be intimate physical contact. Not friendship, not relationship building, just crazy-hot sex. Well, that's not how it works for everybody. Some people want more than a limited-time-only romp, and they're willing to take things slow to get there, including testing their compatibility without getting naked."

"You really think that's how I saw us, Brinn?"

"I wanted us to keep seeing each other after I moved. You didn't."

Forget chilled, now his blood was boiling. "I asked you not to leave. You did."

"I explained why I had to." A muffled sob came through the line. "I don't want our last conversation ever to end in a pointless argument. I wish we could back to the part about the song, and leave it at that."

Their last conversation—ever. Fuck. *Fuck.* "We can do that." He squeezed his eyes closed. Took a breath. "I was on my way home and that country song you like was on the radio. I just wanted you to know I was thinking about you. About every minute we spent together. Best month of my life, Brinn."

"Davis..." she whispered, making no attempt to contain the accompanying sniffles.

"Don't cry, babe. Be happy, like you deserve to be. Fall in love with a good guy who knows how fucking lucky he is, and who's smart enough not to let you go."

"You too—about the happy part."

"I'm going to give it my best shot, count on it."

"Goodbye, Davis."

The line beeped before he could reply. Not his battery or a shitty connection, she'd hung up.

He stared at the screen, watching it until it dimmed,

then faded to black. Turns out he'd called too late after all.

DAVIS

Davis hated driving in Toronto. Hated pretty much everything about the city, actually, including the office building he'd be walking into, as soon as he found a goddamn parking spot.

Fuck it, he'd pay the ridiculous twenty-dollar fee and use the underground lot. If things went well upstairs, twenty bucks would become a laughable amount, not an hour's pay flushed down the drain.

He punched the button on the gate and collected his stub.

Please retain ticket. No exit will be granted without this ticket.

Funny that he'd spent so many years under his family's thumb, wishing he had a ticket to exit their bullshit. Now here he was, about to enter their prized lair—and hoping to hell he wouldn't lose his exit ticket in the process.

He turned his mid-range Honda down the row of spaces closest to the elevator. On the left side, under a bank of bright lights, four gleaming high-end vehicles filled the spaces marked for the partners. Davis Rourke, Senior, Esq. Davis Rourke, Junior, Esq. Sheila Rourke, Esq. Jason Rourke, Esq. Then, an empty space that simply read, *Reserved*.

Since the space would've been his if he hadn't flown the coop six years ago, Davis pulled into the spot. The firm had continued to grow and thrive since his decision to abandon the family business. They didn't need him here. Yet they'd held the spot.

If a member of Brinn's family did something like that, it'd tip the warm-and-fuzzy scales. But this was his family, not the McIntyres. Rourkes didn't do warm and fuzzy. They did cold and calculating. They did control.

He stepped out of the car and shoved the parking stub deep inside his pocket. No way was he losing this ticket.

His dress shoes echoed off the concrete as he headed for the elevator. It arrived quickly, the accompanying *dinging* as its door slid open bouncing off the cavernous walls. At least he had the elevator to himself. Well, aside from his reflection, currently scowling back at him.

The card he was about to play sort of resembled selling out. A thing he never thought he'd do. Especially in regard to his family, and potentially, his career. But it was his last resort at making his idea come to life. The potential outcome outweighed the risks.

The elevator didn't stop until it reached his destination—the fifteenth floor. The mirrored doors slid open and he stepped into the lobby of *Rourke, Rourke & Rourke*. Inwardly, he chuckled. Although both he and his brother had been offered partner status before Davis quit, a fourth *Rourke* hadn't been added to the company name. Jason being the self-centered son-of-a-bitch that he was, the omission had to sting. Maybe fate—that intangible thing Brinn believed in—would give Davis the opportunity to rub the missing *Rourke* in Jason's face. A guy could hope.

He crossed the marble floor to the reception area. Two attractive young women—neither of them familiar —manned an expansive desk. One was engaged on the phone. The second made eye contact as he approached. Dark hair in a tight bun, perfect skin, feminine-yet-professional clothes, practiced smile. Not just somebody who answered phones and fetched coffee, she had "gatekeeper" written all over her.

"Good morning," she said. "How may I help you?"

"I'm here to see Davis Rourke, Senior."

The brunette nodded. "Do you have an appointment?"

"No. But I'm sure he'll see me anyway."

"I'm sorry, sir, but a scheduled appointment is required to see the senior partner. I'm happy to book one for you—I just need your name and the general nature of your business."

"Of course," he said, readying the bomb. "My name is Davis Rourke. The third, to be specific. I'd like to see my grandfather about a personal and professional matter."

The woman's mouth transformed from its measured smile to an *O* shape. The shocked expression disappeared quickly, replaced by her previous, all-business face. "Excuse me while I see if he's available," she said, rising from her post.

Davis nodded. The elegant woman walked down the hall, then knocked on the double doors of his grandfather's corner office. He wasn't surprised that she'd chosen to deliver his message in person. This way, she'd be able to provide a detailed description of the man claiming to be Davis Senior's prodigal grandson.

Though that might be unnecessary. The firm had made plenty of enemies in its time. Undoubtedly more since defending a notorious serial killer a few years back. The entire floor was probably rigged with hidden surveillance cameras. The old man could be checking Davis out this very moment.

The brunette exited the office, closing the doors behind her. "He'll see you now," she said while resuming her perfectly polished guard-dog position behind the reception desk.

"Thanks." Davis had walked these halls more times than he could count. The last time he'd stepped into his grandfather's office had ended with Davis's "fuck this" to a golden opportunity—and his family. Today's meeting ought to be interesting.

He knocked while turning the handle. Directly opposite the door, his grandfather sat behind a massive dark-wood desk. Davis Senior's silver hair contrasted against the back of the black leather chair. He hadn't changed much in six years. At eighty-two, he still looked like the same unshakeable hard-ass with balls of steel Davis had always known. Fucking admirable.

"I see your hair hasn't grown back yet."

Davis laughed and extended his arm across the desk. "It's good to see you too, Gramps."

Davis Senior rose while gripping his grandson's hand for a firm shake. "You're too old to call me that."

"And you're old enough to relax and enjoy it."

"You may be right," his grandfather said as they both settled into chairs. "But I doubt you came all this way to lecture an old man about his workaholic ways. We both know I'm not going to hang up my robes so I can waste the remainder of my life feeding the ducks and playing cards with a bunch of deaf, toothless ninnies."

"Think of the women, Gramps. You'd have your pick of ladies at the Bridge table."

The old man cracked a smile at that. "They couldn't keep up."

No doubt. Age had never factored into his grandfather's activity level. Or his intimate relationships.

"Do your parents know you're here?" The same question he'd asked the day Davis quit the firm.

"No." The same answer too. "My business is with you."

"Then let's hear it."

"I'd like an advance on my inheritance."

"Assuming you still have one coming. A 'heartless bastard who only cares about money, power and his reputation' would've cut you out of the will," his grandfather said, quoting Davis's last visit to this office.

"I disagree. A man like that would want his reputation to remain intact after his death. As much as he wants the world to fear him, he also wants its respect. Cutting his namesake grandson out of the family fortune could be construed as vindictive. Not a quality a powerful, respected man wants marring his legacy."

"A logical deduction."

"Also, you're not that man. I was angry, frustrated and determined to get the hell away from here. I said what was necessary to make that happen."

The founding partner and family patriarch tapped his fingers on the arms of his desk chair. A renowned attorney, he had the ability to wipe all emotion from his expression. The fact that he hadn't done so since Davis walked in the room spoke volumes. He hadn't reached out since Davis walked away that day, but he obviously hadn't written him off, either.

"I have a good job at a nice restaurant. I own a house. I was coasting along, reasonably content with my life, until I met somebody who changed the game. Being with Brinn made me want things I hadn't allowed myself to consider as options. One of those is my own business. I'm an excellent chef. My food is as good or better than the best you've ever eaten—anywhere. I want the freedom to fully explore that, and share it."

"You'd use the advance on your inheritance to open a restaurant."

"Yes. And I'm willing to bet my career it'll be a success."

His grandfather's thick silver eyebrows rose. "An intriguing twist."

"Three years. If the place isn't operating at a healthy profit by the end of three years in business, I'll give it up and come back to the firm. Indefinitely."

A long, low whistle passed through Davis Senior's lips. "Hell of a wager."

"One I'm confident making."

His grandfather's wise eyes stayed focused on Davis's face for a long moment. He pulled a legal pad from the side of his desk, jotted a few lines, signed it with a flourish, then slid it across the desk. "Those are my terms. Take them or leave them."

Davis hadn't expected this to be easy. He turned the pad around and lowered his gaze to the black ink.

An amount equivalent to half your current inheritance will be deposited in your account upon agreement of the following three, non-negotiable conditions, which constitute the sole terms of this contract.

Complimentary dinner once a month, ad infinitum. Invite your parents and brother to the aforementioned dinners. Keep inviting them until they accept.

Gramps

"If your legal skills are rusty and you'd like to have an attorney look that over before you sign," his grandfather said with lawyerly seriousness, "I can have somebody sent down."

"No, I'm good." Davis retrieved a pen from the inside pocket of his suit jacket and added his signature —first name only—to the yellow paper. He met his grandfather's gaze while returning the pad. "You didn't include my offer in the terms of the deal."

"I didn't care for your terms. Since it's my money, I get to dictate the rules."

"Good to know you're still the dictator around here. For a minute, I thought you'd gotten soft."

Gramps barked out a single, gruff laugh. "From the time you were a boy, your parents and I decided that directing you to follow in our footsteps was the right thing. As you matured, you proved us right with your intelligence and quick wit. Traits that'd make you an excellent lawyer. I believed keeping you here, even when it became evident that you hated it, was for the best. A career with the firm would have ensured your success, professionally and financially. But I'd rather have a happy grandson in my life one day a month than a resentful lawyer down the hall every day."

Davis opened his mouth to speak—but was halted by his grandfather's raised hand.

"That's not to say I think you'd have lost your wager. The law may not be in your blood, but it's still

Rourke blood. Your restaurant will be a success, Davis. I'm glad I get to be a part of that."

"So am I."

A few formalities, some catching-up conversation, and a warm handshake later, Davis was on his way down in the elevator. The visit had gone nothing like he'd anticipated. He'd come on the defensive, ready to grovel and barter for money. Sell his soul if necessary. He'd had to do none of those things.

Not only was he leaving with enough cash to implement the business side of his plan, he had a chance to get to know his family from a different angle. Not a bad day. Fate, one might even say. Especially if "one" was a pretty store manager with a dirty mind and an adorable giggle.

Seated in his car, he pulled the phone from his pocket and brought up her contact info. Damn, he was tempted to call. Right now, from the parking garage. Tell her where he was, what he'd just done, and why. That, if not for her, he never would've taken this step. That he owed this rare opportunity to her.

Fate stepped in again, drawing his eye to the time on the dashboard clock. 1:15 on a Monday afternoon. Whether she'd scheduled herself for the opening or closing shift, she'd be at work. No cell phones allowed on the sales floor—one of her rules.

It was for the best. Timing and presentation were key. The element of surprise didn't hurt either. He had one shot at delivering this news, and he sure as hell didn't plan to waste it.

Chapter Twelve

BRINN

MARCH HAD DECIDED TO COME IN LIKE A LION. Outside Brinn's parents' living room window, wind picked up grains of snow, whipped them into a frenzy, then whipped them at the glass. Not a storm—yet. Just general winter nastiness so far.

But she couldn't blame the season for her blah mood. Everything was just...off. And had been since she'd moved. The only truly good thing about her new location was its proximity to her family. The new half-hour drive meant she could visit them more frequently. Once a week, usually. Two, if the weather cooperated with her schedule at the store.

She'd kind of pushed her luck on that front today. However, gambling with the iffy forecast was far more appealing than spending the day alone in her apartment, dwelling on everything lacking in her life.

"You've been nursing that cup of hot chocolate for twenty minutes. You haven't even eaten the marshmallows from the top." Gently, her mom lifted the mug from Brinn's hands and placed it on the coffee table, then settled on the other wing chair by the bay window. "Want to talk about it?"

Brinn shook her head. That didn't stop her mouth from opening, or the words from tumbling out. "The store is making quota every week and my DM is really impressed with my progress there, especially in such a short time. I should be happy, but I feel like I'm just going through the motions. I've always loved working with people, setting goals and accomplishing things. But I can't seem to find the joy or satisfaction anymore, even though I know I'm exceeding expectations."

"What are you going to do about it?" Brinn's mom always supported her. Always loved her wholeheartedly. But she was also always a counselor. She asked questions rather than give suggestions, even when what Brinn wanted most was an opinion, or plain-old motherly directions.

"I don't know. I could look for a new job, I guess."

"Do you think a different job will make you happy? Or will learning the ropes at something new just be a distraction from the real issue?"

"Maybe," she whispered. "Okay, yes. But I don't want to be a needy man-chaser anymore. I want to be like you, Mom. I want a job I enjoy and a happy home with a man I love who can't wait to see me at the end of the day. I know it's dumb, but for that short time we were together, I felt those things with Davis. Now I'm just...gray instead of in color. I'll get over it, I know. Over him. I just haven't figured out how to do that yet. So hit me with your best counseling shtick, because I'll try anything at this point."

Mom sighed, then reached over and squeezed Brinn's hand. "How about some 'Mom' advice instead? Call him back. He's made it clear he wants to see you."

"And then what?"

"Follow your heart."

Brinn snorted. "Because that's worked so well for me in the past."

"Yes, honey, it has." Mom patted her hand, then stood and crossed to the fireplace, where she touched one framed photo after another. Brinn with her dad and the sleigh. Fundraisers she'd organized, community events, college grad, the first store she'd managed. "Look at all the wonderful things that happened when you followed your heart." From behind one of the frames, she picked up a loose photo. "Including this time."

A picture from Christmas Day. Mom had taken it of her and Davis in the kitchen, making turkey dinner. He was so handsome, even with the ridiculous apron on. And she was practically glowing. They didn't look like people who'd only met the night before. They looked like a couple. Two halves of something special.

"May I have that?" she asked when her mom returned to her seat.

"It's yours."

Brinn traced the edge of the print with her fingertips. She had the picture. All the memories too. Now she just needed to decide what to do with them.

BRINN

Crickets chirped inside Brinn's jacket.

"That's got to be you," Zack glanced over from the driver's seat, "because you're the only person in this car with insect noises as a text tone." A minute later, after the reminder tone, he looked over again. "Aren't you going to check it?"

Brinn sighed and pulled the phone from her pocket. She'd look to appease her brother, not because she needed to. Her parents weren't quirky enough to text from the back seat. Zack was driving. The new store was running like a well-oiled machine and her assistant manager was incredibly responsible. Though it could be a casual friend texting out of the blue, Brinn's money was on somebody else. The one person who texted her daily.

She swiped the screen and brought up the incoming message. From Davis, as she'd expected.

> Thinking about you right now.

That's all it said. He always sent a single line, and he didn't bombard her with messages. Just one per day, at random times.

He hadn't called since the night she'd declined his invitation to spend time together. The night she'd told him she might have a date. That was three weeks ago, and it *had* been a date, the first of two with Gary. A nice guy with whom she had lots in common, yet paying attention while he talked had taken conscious effort. Holding his hand and kissing him goodnight had been about as exciting as taking a drink of flat soda.

Going out with Gary had been the kind of thing that should have been good, and might have been, if the timing had been different. If she'd met him before Davis.

He was thinking about her right now? Fine, she had a reply for that.

> I'm always thinking about you.
> Damn you.

Usually, she typed a reply, then deleted it. Sometimes she was weak and hit send. This was one of those times.

"I should block him. Or change my number," she muttered, stuffing the phone back into her pocket.

"If you really didn't want to hear from him, you would've done those things already."

Her head snapped toward her big brother. "I'm not pathetically hanging on, hoping these crumbs turn into a full meal, Zack."

"Look at you, being all metaphorical about the chef." He snorted at the sharp-fingered poke she administered to his shoulder. "I wasn't insulting you, kiddo. I'm saying you haven't given up or cut him off hard because Davis isn't a douche-nozzle like your previous ex. Ex*es*."

"So eloquently put. Your poetic abilities are wasted on real estate listings."

"Yeah, yeah." Zack grinned while issuing a retaliatory brotherly poke to her shoulder. "Let's call a spade a spade. You didn't actually love any of your former boyfriends. You wanted to, but that's all it was—wanting to be in love. With Davis, it was the real deal. Was, and still is. Admit it."

The backseat had gone completely quiet. Brinn looked over her shoulder at two rapt faces. Great, now her parents were in on things.

"Fine, I admit it." She met each of their gazes before turning to face Zack—the instigating pot-stirrer—again. "Now, can we please drop it before we get to the restaurant? I just want to have a nice, relaxing dinner with my favorite people in the world. Jokes and anecdotes only from here out. I don't think I can handle any more deep, emotional discussions on this subject. Please?"

Zack gave her a single nod. "Shallow and superficial are my specialties when it comes to dinner conversation. Ask any of the women I've dated."

"Or his parents," Mom chimed in from the backseat.

Laughter pushed away the weightiness of the previous moment. Brinn flopped back against the plush upholstery of Zack's old-man sedan, closing her eyes as the late-afternoon sunshine streamed through the glass. This is what she needed—quality time with people she loved, in the only place that'd ever felt like home. Aside from Davis's house. But that had nothing to do with the house or its location, and everything to do with its occupant.

She sighed and opened her eyes, just in time to see Zack turn into an empty parking lot in front of an equally vacant building. "Checking the locks after a viewing?" she asked when he parked in front of the main entrance.

Zack never trusted other agents to properly close up after showing his listings. The places that still had residents or tenants weren't such a big deal, but an unoccupied property with an unsecured door had the potential for all kinds of unpleasantness. Even in a smaller city.

"Actually, the place is sold. The new owner asked me to drop something off before dinner. Hope you don't mind."

"No, of course not."

"Great. Let's go," he said, removing the keys from the ignition, then unbuckling his seat belt.

"You need me to go in with you?" Kind of odd, but she followed his lead and exited the car. "Are you delivering something heavy?" she asked while walking around toward the trunk.

Zack looked her up and down. "I don't think so." He threw a big-brotherly arm around her shoulders and steered her toward the door. "Pretty sure the owner would agree. Let's find out."

"Now you're freaking me out." With each step they took toward the blacked-out glass door, her heart beat faster and harder. "Tell me you didn't set up some weird blind date. Especially not with a guy who'd think it was fun to meet me in an empty automotive dealership."

"Okay," he said, pulling the door and nudging her through the opening. "I won't tell you that."

The door closed behind her, with Zack on the opposite side. But she wasn't alone in the building. Davis stood beside a candlelit table for two in the middle of the old showroom. Hands stuffed in the pockets of his black suit pants, separating the bottom of the matching jacket, he was more delicious than the aroma from whatever food he'd prepared. More than anything, she wanted to run across the room. Fling herself into the arms she knew would catch and hold her.

"What is this?" she asked, holding her ground near the door.

"Sunday dinner."

She turned at the sound of Zack's engine starting—then fading away. "Oh my god, they left. I can't believe they did that." She spun on her heel and speared Davis with a look. "They know how things ended between us. How I've felt since..."

"Since we said goodbye."

"Yes." She swallowed the lump that'd formed in her throat. "How did you convince them to be part of," she waved her hands at the massive room with its covered windows and small, single table in the center, "whatever this is?"

"Easily." Casually as anything, he made the distance between them disappear. A matter of inches separated them. He kept his hands in his pockets, but his gaze wandered over her hair and face like a soft caress. "I called, then I went to see them. I told them what I wanted to do and they agreed to help make it happen."

"Make what happen?" The whispered words had barely left her lips when the impact of Zack's comments hit her. She gasped, gaped up at Davis. "Zack was talking about you. *You* bought this place?"

"I did. With an advance on my inheritance."

"You've been in touch with your family?" That in itself was monumental. Even without everything else that was happening.

"Just my grandfather so far. I went to his office prepared for the worst, but that's not what happened. He was glad to see me. I'd even say he's missed me.

And to my surprise, the feelings turned out to be mutual."

"Wow. That's wonderful. I think so, anyway."

"I do too. And it's because of you. I had all that stuff locked away where it couldn't get to me anymore. Then you happened. You're like a walking, talking, so-fucking-beautiful-inside-and-out-it-takes-my-breath-away key. You made me want things I'd sworn off forever."

She felt her mouth moving, but nothing came out. All she could do was blink up at him and wait for whatever might be next.

"Then I came to see your brother. We looked at a bunch of properties and decided on this one. He's very good at his job. I'm going to enlist him to find a house too, if you're okay with that."

"Why wouldn't I be? You know I have no animosity toward you. If you want to hire my brother, that's your business."

"No, babe. It's *our* business." He gathered her restless, twisting hands and brought them to his lips. Then he released them and cupped her face in his palms. "I don't want the life I had before you. I want a life with you in it. Every day, here at the restaurant. Every night, when it's time to go home."

"You want me to quit my job and come work for you?"

"Hell no. I want you as my partner in this business." A smile tugged at the corners of his sexy mouth. "I only want to be the boss when we're alone and naked. In our bedroom."

How could she not melt at that? But she couldn't just jump into his arms. Not with so much hanging in the balance. "What would you want from me?"

"In the bedroom? Long list, babe."

"Not there."

"Damn," he said, winking as one of his irresistible grins settled into place on his handsome face.

She giggled in spite of herself, grabbing fistfuls of his suit jacket and tugging him closer. "In the business. Seriously. What you're suggesting is...beyond huge. I don't have money to invest. I've never used my diploma to actually manage a restaurant. Plus...what if *we* don't work out?"

"I do accept manual and oral forms of payment."

"What about penetrative?" she asked, copying the rest of their conversation from Boxing Day.

"Oh yeah. As long as I'm on the penetrating end and the transaction is with you." His grin changed to a softer smile. "Forget about the money, Brinn, it's covered. And yeah, there's going to be a learning curve. For both of us. But with your excellence in people-management and my skill set in the kitchen, we've got a solid foundation to get started. As for the last question...we'll be equal partners. If you want out at some point, you'll be entitled to half the business." He stroked her cheek and lips, his gaze never straying from her eyes. "But you'll walk away with one-hundred percent of my heart."

Her heart was ready to leap out of her chest. "I've missed you," she whispered. "So much."

He took that as permission to kiss her. And oh god, what a kiss. Firm pressure from his soft lips, the teasing sweep of his tongue, the hum of something electric and magical racing through her body. Mistake or not, she wrapped her arms around him and got as close as possible. Held him tight even when they had to come up for air.

"You're ruining me again," she said.

"Good. Because I don't plan to let you go this time." He slid his hand down her back, using her ass to pull her tighter. "I know some people would say it's too soon, but we're great together. I don't want to waste another day or night without you in my life. I love you, Brinn."

"I love you too. I feel like I always have."

"Be with me. Here. Let's build something incredible together."

This time, when she glanced around the building, it struck her as something loaded with potential, not a big empty space. "It'll be an amazing restaurant. I can already picture it full of happy customers."

"With the two of us working on it, yeah, it will be." His strong-yet-gentle fingers caught her chin and tipped it upward. "But I wasn't talking about the restaurant. I was talking about us. There's something for you in my left pocket."

Butterflies whirred to life in her stomach as she lifted the flap and slid her hand inside his pocket. Her fingers connected with a small box.

"Hope you're not disappointed," he said, as she carefully removed it, then lifted the top, revealing a single fortune cookie.

"With you, never." With shaking hands, she cracked the cookie open. Pulled the strip of paper free and smoothed it between her fingers.

Stay.

Same message as the last fortune, but she wouldn't give the same answer.

"That's it, Brinn. One cookie. One question."

One cookie was all she needed. One dream come true. One man to share the love of a lifetime.

She bit her bottom lip, but it was pointless. There was no holding back the massive smile that stretched so wide, it probably connected her ears. "Yes. There's nowhere in the world I'd rather be than here, with you. Always and every day, yes."

Epilogue

DAVIS

"BABE," DAVIS CALLED FROM THE OFFICE HE shared with Brinn. "Can you come in here for a minute?"

"I'm coming."

He snagged her by the waist when she stepped through the doorway. Pressed her against the wall with her hands above her head. "Not yet, you're not." He unzipped her pants with his free hand and slid his fingers inside her panties. "But I can make it a reality in about sixty seconds."

"That long? You must be spending—" Her breath hitched as he rubbed circles over her clit. "Too much time in the—oh god—kitchen and not enough in—" She arched toward his touch, shaking and panting as he gave her the pressure and speed she needed. "Oh god, Davis…"

He released her arms, which instantly wrapped around his neck. "Want to finish that statement?"

Her soft hair tickled his neck as she shook her head. "Nope. Happily proven wrong." She snuggled in with her cheek pressed to his chest. "Working together certainly has its perks."

"That it does. Speaking of work…" He kissed her forehead, then led her by the hand to her desk chair. "I need you to check the bookings for the banquet room. A guy I know from way back is hoping we have an opening around Christmas. On a weekend. I know it's a crazy request at this point, but he has something special in the works and he really needs our room for it."

"Sneaky. Using your powers of orgasmification on me so you could hit me up for what's most likely an impossible task." She rolled her chair beneath the desk and tapped at the keyboard until a spreadsheet he didn't understand and didn't want to understand popped into place on her screen. "I hope you didn't promise anything," she said, scrolling through the multicolored squares. "We've been booked solid for the holidays since early September."

"Yeah, that's amazing."

"No, it's not. Everybody knows 'Rare' has the best food. It's the place to be, period." She smiled up at him, blue eyes shining with love and admiration the likes of which he couldn't have imagined two years ago.

"It's not just the food. Without a great manager handling everything beyond the kitchen walls, I'd be lucky to fill a handful of tables per night. This place would still be a pipedream without you."

"We do make a great team." She leaned up from her seat to kiss him. "Okay, let me have another look at this schedule."

He kept his poker face in place while leaning over the side of her chair. If it didn't work out this way, he'd come up with another plan. But he wasn't putting it off. Especially not after what he'd discovered this morning.

"Oh my god, I can't believe I did that. I have Dr. Jensen's office party booked on two separate dates. I swear something is sucking my brain power lately." She adjusted her spreadsheet, then pointed at a red square on her monitor. "Saturday the twenty-third. The day before Christmas Eve. Do you think that'll work?"

Fucking right, it'd work. Pretty damn perfectly. "Yeah, definitely."

"Great. Name for the reservation?" she asked, her pink-lacquered nails poised over the keyboard.

"Let me give you his card." Davis pulled the lone business card from his back pocket. "I know he can't wait to hear from you."

An adorable wrinkle formed near the bridge of her nose when he held out the card. "Davis, that's *your* card..." Her bottom lip dropped and her eyes went wide as saucers when he pressed it onto her palm—while going down on one knee. "Oh my god," she whispered, turning the card over to reveal the ring taped to the back. "What is this?"

"I was going to do this when we celebrated Rare's anniversary back in August. But I didn't want this moment to get lost in the commotion of the other. So I planned to wait until we were alone Christmas Eve. The perfect day to make this all about us. Only now it's about more than that, and I'm going out of my mind trying to keep calm and have patience, but I can't wait another minute." He pulled the rose-gold ring from beneath the clear tape and slid it on her finger. "Marry me, Brinn. This Christmas. Make me the happiest, fucking luckiest, man in the world."

"Oh my god, you know, don't you?" she whispered.

"That we're going to be a table for three sometime next year? Yeah, baby, I know. I found the pregnancy test in the garbage can."

"But I shoved it way down to the bottom."

"Which is where I found it when I went searching—after seeing the flattened box on the top of the recycling container."

"I'm sorry." A fat tear broke free of her glassy eyes and rolled down her cheek. "I'm messing everything up. The bookings, hiding the test, getting pregnant…"

Shit, not how he'd expected this to go. "The mistake in the bookings was fate giving us an opening. Just like my house getting robbed on Christmas Eve two years ago. You've always sucked at trying to hide things from me, so that one doesn't even count. As for getting pregnant—I get to take half the credit for that, and there's nothing messed up about it."

"Yes, there is. I took antibiotics after I sliced my hand open in the kitchen. I didn't even think about the effect on my birth control pills. There are always warning labels on prescriptions, but I didn't read them."

"*Our* birth control pills. And I'm the one that picked up the medication after your stitches. I could've read the labels too, but I didn't. You don't get to shoulder this, Brinn."

She swiped at another tear. "A baby wasn't in the plan."

"Fuck the plan."

"I believe fucking is how we fucked up the plan in the first place."

So goddamn adorable. He pulled her onto his knee and captured her mouth, teasing his tongue inside, then groaning as she sucked it between her warm lips. "You're wearing my ring and carrying my child, but you still haven't answered me," he said when she pulled back, glassy eyed and breathing hard.

"Did so." She held him for support while stretching to retrieve something from her top drawer. "The day you gave me this." She opened her palm to reveal a thin strip of paper bearing his handwriting. *Stay.* "It was yes then and it's yes now. It'll always be yes with you."

"I'm going to hold you to that, my beautiful, sexy future wife." He stood, scooping her up with him. "We've got half an hour until the prep staff gets here. And I've got plans for every one of those thirty minutes."

"Then you'd better get started, future husband." A naughty smile curved her pretty mouth as she wiggled out of her pants and unbuttoned her blouse. "You're running down the clock."

Thank you for reading GIFT WRAPPED!

Join Karla's mailing list to stay up to date
on all her books & news:
www.karladoyle.com/newsletter

Want more sexy and sweet Christmas romance? You're going to love 12 DAYS, Kelly and Adeline's best friends to lovers story!

12 DAYS

Kelly Horne and Adeline Mission have been best friends
since the third grade. Yes, he thinks she's pretty.
And hot. Smart. Funny. But they're buds. Roommates.
End of story.

Until he opens a package delivered to his house without
checking the name on the label, and finds Addie has
ordered a vibrating cock ring for some guy who doesn't
deserve her, because no guy does.

There's a gift receipt in the box, meaning she intends to
give the sex toy to somebody for Christmas...in 12 days.

12 days to undo a lifetime of "just friends".
12 days to change the name she writes on that gift tag.
12 days to win the girl he just realized
has always been the one for him.

. . .

Turn the page to read the first chapter of 12 Days.

Chapter One

December 13

KELLY

"A delivery van just stopped in front of your house," his buddy, Rick, called from the living room. "Guy's walking up to your door."

"Can you grab it? My hands are covered in rib sauce."

"On it."

From the kitchen, Kelly Horne heard the groaning creak of floorboards under Rick's feet, the agonized squeak of the front door's hinges as it opened. He needed to give the old house some TLC before it was too late.

A bit more squeaking and creaking brought Rick to the kitchen, where he set a brown package on the counter. "That's a small box. I'm guessing this is something for one of the chicks in your current rotation."

"I don't have a rotation."

Rick's thick eyebrows rose. "Are you telling me the horndog never humps the same bitch twice?"

"Classy," he said, shaking his head. "You're lucky that Addie's not here. If she heard you referring to women as bitches to be humped, you might as well book yourself an appointment to get neutered." He made a snip-snip motion with his fingers, grinning when his buddy instinctively covered his junk.

Fair payback for the horndog reference. He hadn't minded the nickname that played on his last name back in their high-school days, but at thirty-one, he was ready for the tag to roll over and play dead. He still had no problem getting action, but he did so with more discretion and a much higher skill level. The old horndog had learned a lot of tricks since high school.

He pointed at the tray of gooey ribs before turning to the sink to wash his hands. "Make yourself useful and stick that pan back in the oven."

"On it." Rick joked around about many things, but never food. "Anything else I can do?"

"Yeah. The baby greens, diced cucumbers, and light raspberry vinaigrette are in the fridge, waiting to be mixed up." He watched Rick's expression sour at the mention of healthy food, then hit him with a prime punchline. "What, don't like the idea of tossing my salad?"

Rick's eyebrows drew together briefly, before rising so high, they looked as if they were trying to escape his grumpy face. "You're one sick son of a bitch."

"Watch what you say about my mother." Kelly grinned, scooping the plain, brown box from the counter. He'd done a bunch of online shopping this holiday season, but he had no idea what was in this particular package. "On the subject of my mother, let's find out what I can't remember buying for her."

"You do that. I'm grabbing my beer. Need to cleanse my palette." Still sporting a disturbed expression, Rick shook his head. "You're lucky I don't actually eat salad, since you just ruined it for me forever."

Kelly laughed, busting the packing tape while watching his buddy head into the living room. "Sorry, man. Messing with you is just too easy."

"You'd know about easy," Rick shot back, reentering the kitchen, beer in hand. "On that note, you could leave somebody in town untouched. Take pity on those of us who don't have the Kelly Horne magic."

"I haven't been with every woman in Hope Harbor."

"True. You haven't sealed the deal with Adeline." Rick knocked back a swig from his bottle of Bud Light, grinning as he wiped his mouth with the back of his hand. "Must suck to be around her every single day and know you're never going to get some Missionary."

"Hey." Kelly froze with his hand curled around the packing paper surrounding the box's contents. "Don't call her that."

"Relax, *Dad*. It's a joke."

Shit, should he tell or not tell? He weighed the options on a scale of how much would it hurt Addie, gritted his teeth and made a choice. "Look, it's a joke to you, but I know for a fact that she hates that old nickname. She might laugh it off with you, but on the inside, it makes her feel bad. So...just lay off with her, okay? She's not a dirty-minded pig, like we are."

"But apparently your mom *is*," Rick said, his bug-eyed gaze zoned in to Kelly's hands.

He followed suit and looked down at the item he'd absentmindedly unwrapped. "What the fuck?"

"More like, *how* to fuck." Laughter erupted from Rick's mouth when Kelly tossed the item into the sink as if it were on fire. "That's like, whoa. How'd that conversation go? *What do you want for Christmas, Mom? Well, son, a cock ring would be nice.*"

"That's disgusting, even for you." Kelly snagged his buddy's beer and drained the remainder of the bottle.

Hands raised in surrender, Rick approached the sink. "All right, all right, I'm sorry. Obviously, you didn't get your mom a cock ring for Christmas." Despite the apologetic tone and words, his grin stretched wider. "You bought it for yourself. Interesting choice," he said, inspecting the plastic-wrap-encased sex toy. "I would've had to buy one with a bigger ring, but we can't all be so well-endowed."

Kelly grunted. "You wish. Also, I didn't order that. For me or anybody. It's a mistake."

"A pretty fucking wild one." Rick snapped his fingers. "Hey, maybe it wasn't the seller who made the mistake. Maybe the delivery guy got the address mixed up."

"You didn't check the label when you brought it in?"

Rick shook his head. "Didn't figure I needed to. I've

never gotten a wrong package at my place, or had one of mine go missing."

"You'd better hope the address is way off, because if this package was supposed to go to one of my neighbors, I'm going to be picturing them using that damn cock ring every time I see them."

"In that case, I hope it was meant for the old people who are always at your door, bringing you baked goods and prayer meeting invitations," Rick said, racing Kelly to the empty box on the counter, and beating him by a fraction of a second. Jerkhole that he could be, Rick covered the label with his hand, blocking it from Kelly's view.

Kelly scowled while Rick's face lit up brighter than the Christmas lights Addie had strung throughout the house. "It's the old fogies, isn't it? Shit. I don't want to think about wrinkled people having sex."

"Oh, it's not them you're going to be picturing." Rick lifted his hand, then turned the box toward Kelly. "That vibrating cock ring belongs to your roommate. Or, to the guy she's giving it to, if you want to be technical. Looks like sweet little Missionary has outgrown her old nickname."

"Give me that." The bottom dropped out of Kelly's stomach as he read the shipping label at close range. *Adeline B. Mission, 152 St. Henry Street, Hope Harbor.* "This can't be right. They must've sent her the wrong item."

"Or, maybe it's totally right, and the sex swing she ordered to go with it is being shipped separately." Rick howled with laughter while ducking Kelly's punch. "Just saying, I was here when she asked you about putting a hook in the ceiling, near her bed."

"For a swag lamp she saw at Ikea."

"Uh-huh. Sure it was."

"Addie's not into sex toys."

Rick's eyebrows rose. "You sound pretty sure of that. Have you been snooping through your tenant's room, Mr. Landlord?"

"No. Never. I just know she's not into that kind of thing."

"You just know it." Rick barked out a laugh when Kelly nodded. "All right, then. Hope there's a quiet little corner waiting in your land of denial, because I have a feeling there's going to be a lot of noise from the room next to yours, once Adeline puts that ring on her man's dick. Who's the guy, anyway? Somebody we know?"

The front door's telltale squeak replaced any answer Kelly could've given. "Shit, she's home. We've got less than a minute before she's in here."

"I'll grab the packing paper," Rick said, scrambling.

"Hello..." Addie called from the front hall.

"Hey. In the kitchen with Rick, making dinner. Hope you've got an appetite."

Rick snorted. "Oh, I'd say she does. Just not for ribs."

"Shut up." Kelly shot him a glare, his gaze snagging on the invoice in the bottom of the open box as he pushed the flaps open. Unable to resist, he picked it up.

Not a regular receipt, a gift receipt—meaning, whomever she'd bought the cock ring for didn't know about it yet.

"What are you smiling about?"

"Nothing." He returned the receipt to its place and nodded at the item in Rick's hand. "Quick, put it in the box."

"That's what Addie's going to be saying."

"What am I going to be saying?" Addie asked, entering the kitchen.

"Hey." Kelly ignored the question while subtly tucking the package behind his back. "Busy day at the store?"

Her dark-brown hair shimmered with her nod. "Mostly with poinsettias. I can't seem to keep enough in stock."

"That's awesome." Standing shoulder-to-shoulder with his partner in postal crime, he passed the box to Rick. If his buddy could get out of the room without Addie seeing the package, they could tape it closed and she'd be the none the wiser about their accidental invasion of her privacy.

She shrugged. "Selling Christmas poinsettias pays the bills, but it's a boring day when that's all I'm doing. Now, back to *my* question. I distinctly heard Rick say, 'That's what Addie's going to be saying,' when I walked in, and the two of you currently look guilty as sinners on Sunday."

"You got me," Rick said. "We were talking about the

ribs Kelly's making and how you're going to eat all of them, if we don't get to them first."

Emotion flashed across Addie's expressive face, ending with her soft-pink lips in a downward curve.

Shit, he knew that look. He'd seen it many times over the years. She'd interpreted Rick's comment—lie that it was—as him calling her an overeater. Something that'd been true earlier in her life. A habit she'd worked damn hard to break as an adult. He wouldn't let her feel like crap to cover his idiot mistake.

"Rick wasn't talking about food." He stepped away from his buddy and held out his hand.

Rick shot him a *what-the-fuck* look, shaking his head as he surrendered the box. "It's your funeral."

Better that than causing Addie any hurtful emotions. Something she should never have to feel.

"The truth is, Rick accepted a delivery while I was adding more sauce to the ribs. I've bought a bunch of stuff online for Christmas and I opened it without checking the label. Turns out, it wasn't mine, it's yours. I thought if Rick and I could get it back in the box and sealed up before you saw it, you wouldn't be embarrassed about ordering—"

"A cock ring," Rick said, grinning ear-to-ear. "With nine vibration modes, according to the tag. Nice job, Missionary. Or should I say, not-so-Missionary. Who's the lucky dude?"

"You don't have to answer him." He extended his

arm and offered the package. "Sorry for unintentionally invading your privacy."

In the twenty-three years he'd known Addie, her face had never been as red as this moment. She stood across from them, wide-eyed gaze flitting back and forth between them, lips moving, no words coming out. Only a strangled squeak, before she grabbed the box and darted from the kitchen. Two rooms over, her door closed with a bang.

"Wow, you really fucked that up."

"*I* fucked it up?" Kelly whirled to face Rick. "I was going to say she'd ordered something personal or maybe, *maybe,* say a sex toy. You're the one who jumped in with the detailed description. 'Nine vibrations modes.' What the fuck was that about? *And* you called her that damn nickname I had just told you not to use."

"Geez, Grandpa. Pull your giant wedgie out of your crack and relax. Adeline knows it was just teasing. *Good* teasing. I complimented her, in case you missed that. She's awesome and gorgeous. It's about time she loosened up and lived a little. I'm glad she's found somebody she wants to get down-and-dirty with, aren't you?" Rick opened the fridge and leaned inside, the clinking of bottles punctuating the silence in the kitchen. A couple seconds later, Rick popped up, staring Kelly down from behind the open door. "Holy fuck, it's finally happening."

"No idea what you're talking about."

"Yeah, you do. Even if you aren't ready to admit it

yet." Rick shut the fridge with his foot, then passed Kelly a beer. "You're not happy that Adeline's giving some guy a cock ring for Christmas. You're jealous."

"Not jealous. Concerned." He twisted off the cap and made a perfect, three-point shot into the trash can across the room. "I haven't met the guy. She hasn't talked about anybody. He might be a complete asshole."

"Or he might not be. Adeline's a smart girl. She's not going to give it up to someone who's not worthy."

"Nobody's worthy." The comment left his mouth before he could rein it in. "None of the schmucks from around here, anyway."

"Maybe the guy's from out of town. Somebody she met through her business. Or online."

Shit, that possibility was even worse. Kelly could check up on guys he knew. Threaten their very existence if they caused Addie even a second's worth of pain. But if he didn't know the secret guy in her life, he had no control. He needed information. All of it, and soon.

"You want to play some poker tonight?" Rick's question snapped Kelly back to the present. "Because I could use some extra cash, and your face isn't hiding shit at the moment."

"I don't know what you're talking about."

"Bullshit, you don't. It's killing you that she's into somebody. You're jealous of cock-ring guy."

He shot Rick the middle finger, then took a long pull

from his beer to mask whatever his buddy thought he could see there.

Addie was his best friend. Had been since the third grade, when he moved into this house with his parents and became her neighbor. She'd jumped to his defense that first day at a new school, threatening to sit on anyone who heckled him for having "a girl's name." They'd had each other's backs every single day since.

He wasn't jealous, he was being protective. Of course, he wanted her to be happy. It didn't bother him at all to think of her with somebody else.

Smiling at some guy, laughing at his jokes. Kissing him. Getting naked with him.

He turned to the sink and spat his mouthful of beer. "Rancid," he said, dumping the perfectly good lager down the drain. "Grab me another one."

"Sure." Rick retrieved another cold one and handed it over. "Don't you hate it when something goes off before you have a chance to enjoy it? Something you assumed would always be there, waiting for you to have it, whenever you decided you wanted it?"

"Yeah, I'm devastated by the loss of one beer. How will I ever recover?" He cracked the top and clinked his bottle against Rick's. "By enjoying a different beer, that's how." That's how he'd get past this weird blip in his chest about Addie, too. His little black book had never let him down before. This time shouldn't be any different.

Shouldn't be, but he already knew that it was. He

had no desire to send Rick packing so he could message a sure-thing to come over. He wanted to get rid of Rick and focus on one woman, that much was true. But not some handpicked hookup. Addie. And not for a laidback night of snacks and sitcoms. More. Much more.

"Time's up," Rick said, pulling Kelly from thoughts he'd never seen coming.

The buzzer had gone off. Time was up for the ribs in the oven, but not for him. He glanced at the fridge, where Addie's colorful, botanical calendar hung from an equally flowery magnet. Stuff he wouldn't have thought to choose but couldn't imagine his kitchen without.

Christmas was twelve days away. Twelve days to undo a lifetime of "just friends" with Addie. Twelve days to change the name she wrote on that gift's tag. Twelve days to win the girl he just realized has always been the one for him.

12 DAYS is available now in ebook and paperback!

Also by Karla Doyle

Last Call Casanova (Hope Harbor)

Fleshing It Out (Hope Harbor)

The Deal With Love (Hope Harbor)

Doggy Style (Hope Harbor)

Resorting to Love (linked to Hope Harbor)

White Lie Christmas (linked to Hope Harbor)

King of Her Dreams (Hope Harbor)

Heart of Texas (linked to Hope Harbor)

Her Pipe Dream (Hope Harbor)

12 Days (Hope Harbor)

Puck That

Shifting Gears (Under the Hood)

Driver's Seat (Under the Hood)

Gingerbread Man (Man of the Month: Candy Cane Key)

Just in Queso (Man of the Month: Magnolia Point)

Unexpected Addition

Dating the Doubter

Gift Wrapped

Cup of Sugar (Close to Home #1)

Icing on the Cake (Close to Home #2)

Sweet as Candy (Close to Home #3)

Body of Work (Very Personal Training #1)

Worth the Wait (Very Personal Training #2)

Game Plan

More Than Words

Crossing the Line

Visit Karla's website for the most up-to-date list.

www.karladoyle.com

Click here to see Karla's books sorted by tropes and themes!

www.karladoyle.com/books/by-tropes/

About the Author

 A small-town girl with some big-city experience, Karla resides in Southwestern Ontario with her husband and two amazing, young-adult kids. She studied fashion design in college and spent 20+ years working in that industry before succumbing to the writing muse. When she's not writing the sexy stories that swirl around in her head, you can find her spending time with family, hanging out with book-loving friends on Facebook, or cuddled up with a book and her adorable pets.

Karla loves hearing from readers! Email her at: karla@karladoyle.com.

Join Karla's mailing list to stay up to date on all her news: www.karladoyle.com/newsletter

Connect with Karla online:

- facebook.com/KarlaDoyleAuthor
- instagram.com/KarlaDoyleAuthor
- tiktok.com/@karladoyleauthor
- bookbub.com/authors/karla-doyle
- goodreads.com/karlad
- youtube.com/@KarlaDoyleAuthor
- bsky.app/profile/karladoyleauthor.bsky.social
- patreon.com/KarlaDoyleAuthor

Even with editing, sometimes mistakes slip through. If you find one, please email the author so she can have it corrected.

karla@karladoyle.com